"Get 'em, boys, kill 'em good!"
went up the cry . . .

"Jump!" Stine called, already in the air. He barely reached the top of the car in the train alongside Villalobos's. Slocum followed more easily, but he fell to his knees. Before he recovered, he heard the sharp command from the direction of the engine.

"Kill them!"

A shot tore through the air next to Slocum's head. He ducked involuntarily. As he went into a crouch, his hand closed around his Colt Navy. He drew, located the man shooting at him and fired three times. One of the rounds knocked the man from the top of the other car. His attacker yelped in pain, dropped his gun, and flailed about as he fell off.

"We've got to get out of here," Slocum said, spinning around and crashing into Stine and another man locked in a deadly fight. The trio fell to the top of the freight car and rolled over and over. The man held a rifle and discharged it.

Stine yelled in pain, fingers burned on the metal barrel. As he released his grip, the man he fought tried to get the muzzle lowered and shoved into Stine's gut. Slocum swung his six-gun and caught the man above the right eye, sending him to the ground.

JAKE LOGAN

RAILROAD TO HELL

JOVE BOOKS, NEW YORK

This is a work of fiction. Names, characters, places, and incidents are either the product of the author's imagination or are used fictitiously, and any resemblance to actual persons, living or dead, business establishments, events, or locales is entirely coincidental.

RAILROAD TO HELL

A Jove Book / published by arrangement with
the author

PRINTING HISTORY
Jove edition / July 2001

The Penguin Putnam Inc. World Wide Web site address is
www.penguinputnam.com

ISBN: 0-515-13102-4

A JOVE BOOK®
Jove Books are published by The Berkley Publishing Group,
a division of Penguin Putnam Inc.,
375 Hudson Street, New York, New York 10014.
JOVE and the "J" design
are trademarks belonging to Penguin Putnam Inc.

PRINTED IN THE UNITED STATES OF AMERICA

10 9 8 7 6 5 4 3 2 1

1

John Slocum had seen it all before and wanted no part of the fight. He moved to the far end of the bar, taking his cracked mug of flat, warm beer with him. He had paid a good nickel for that beer and wasn't going to abandon the tepid brew because of a barroom fight. Sipping at the bitter beer, he watched the two antagonists square off.

He had no idea what the fight was about, and it didn't matter to him as long as everyone left him alone. Being on the trail for over a month had taken its toll on him, especially since he'd lost a good friend to cholera along the way. Little Ben had been anything but little—he had been a mountain of gristle and bone and Slocum had never found a more decent partner. That made it doubly painful when this robust, hearty man had fallen not to a bullet or Indian arrow, but to bad water.

The indignity of his death had left Slocum more than a mite bitter, and when he rode into Denver he wanted no part of civilization or any of the amenities it offered. Those included the women milling around the dance hall, making bets on the two men and blatantly offering their bodies to the winner, whichever of the two battling cowboys that might be.

"Take it back," shouted the man farthest from Slocum. "You got no call sayin' a thing like that."

"Eat my lead, you stupid son of a bitch," said the man with his back to Slocum.

"You ain't got the guts to throw down on me. I—" The other man barely got the words out of his mouth when the man nearest to Slocum drew. His speed was good, but the other man was faster and was going for his own hog-leg as he spoke.

The pair exchanged rounds. The man nearest Slocum died without so much as a gulp, but his antagonist across the room wasn't killed outright. The man staggered up to the bar, clutching his belly. His six-shooter fired, shattering the large mirror behind the counter. Turning slowly, he fired again and again, wildly, into the crowd. The women began screaming, and the men dived under the tables for what cover they could find.

"You, you done kilt me," the man gasped out, pulling himself along the bar. Slocum sipped at his beer, then set it down when it became obvious to him the man was speaking to him.

"You killed the man who insulted you," Slocum said. "We've got no quarrel, mister. I don't want anything but to finish my beer and drift on."

"You cain't get out of apologizing like that, you lily-livered cayuse!" Another shot ripped through the now silent dance hall. This time the wood wall inches from Slocum's head exploded into splinters. He flinched when one cut his cheek.

"I see that you wouldn't take my apology, even if I offered one," Slocum said. He stared smack down the barrel of the man's six-gun at death.

"Damn right I wouldn't."

The man's finger turned white on the trigger, showing he was going to fire again. Slocum never gave him the chance. His hand flashed to the ebony handle of the Colt

Navy in its cross-draw holster, pulled the trusty six-shooter out, and got off a single shot before the man could fire.

Slocum's slug caught the man in the middle of the face, knocking him back. The man's gun hand rose, and the shot discharged harmlessly into the ceiling. A small cascade of plaster came down on him, hinting at how dirt would soon be shoveled over the man's corpse.

Slocum returned his six-shooter to his holster and took a deep breath. He ought to have stayed on the trail. He wasn't headed anywhere in particular, but that was better than being in a dance hall when he was suffering under his current mood. He wasn't going to take squat off any man, much less a drunk waving around a gun.

"Excuse me, mister," came a deep voice. "You have the look of a man who could use a real drink. It'd be my pleasure to buy you some whiskey. And if you're inclined, come on and join us in a little game of poker."

Slocum knew the law would be swarming into the dance hall to see what the ruckus was about. He nodded curtly, went across the large, smoke-filled room and sank down to an empty chair. Good as his word, the man pushed a half-filled bottle of rotgut across to him.

"The name's Abel Stine," the man said. Slocum liked it that he didn't shove out his hand to be shaken, sensing Slocum's mood. Sizing up the man wasn't too hard. He spent his time outdoors, had a sturdy look to him that showed he didn't ride a horse or chase cattle as much as he did something else—maybe he was a miner. Stine's broad shoulders and powerful arms hinted at that. But he was also weather-beaten and leathery, as if he spent more than his share of time out in the noonday sun.

"You work a railroad?" Slocum asked.

Stine's eyes narrowed as he peered at Slocum. "How'd you know that?"

Slocum shrugged it off. "A good guess."

"You don't have the look of a man accustomed to guessing," Stine said.

"I'm not inclined to admit being wrong," Slocum countered. He took a drink, then picked up the cards as a squad of Denver's finest policemen burst into the saloon.

They bustled about and questioned people, a pair of scarred veterans coming over to glare at Slocum and Stine and his friends.

"What went on? How come those two got killed?" demanded the burlier of the pair, tapping a nightstick across his palm with loud swacking sounds. He obviously wanted to apply the stick to someone's head. Slocum shifted slightly so he could reach his six-shooter again, but Stine spoke up.

"Me and the boys was playin' some poker when we heard the gunshots. Looks to me like those two killed each other."

"That's all you saw?"

"Well, there's something more," Stine said, staring across the table at Slocum. Brown eyes locked with Slocum's green ones. "I think this galoot is cheatin' me at cards. He's won the last three hands."

"Don't draw to inside straights if you don't want me taking advantage of you," Slocum said.

The policemen snarled something about railroaders Slocum didn't quite understand, then moved on. Five minutes later, after downing almost a whole bottle of free whiskey given them by the barkeep, the police dragged the bodies from the dance hall, satisfied the two had killed each other.

"Coppers," grumbled Stine. He took a deep breath, then said, "Your deal, mister."

"Slocum, John Slocum." He shuffled the cards and dealt a hand of draw poker. Slocum didn't have much more than a couple dimes to bet, but he won a few small pots and was soon several dollars ahead. He found the rhythm of the cards, the soft slip of the pasteboards, the thrill of the gambling was exactly what he needed to take his mind off his problems. For the first time in weeks he did not lament the loss of Little Ben or worry that he had no clear destination in front of him.

Then came a moment of decision he had not anticipated. Looking at the full house, kings over tens, he stood to win a pot with more than fifty dollars in it. The play went around until he had to pony up an IOU, which Stine gladly accepted.

Slocum had played enough to know Stine was bluffing, pushing him further and further with what had to be a punk hand.

"You in or out, Slocum?" Stine asked.

Slocum double-checked his intuition of his own winning hand. Stine wore a small knitted cap pulled down almost to his ears. When he bluffed he occasionally touched the edge of the cap, running his fingers along it. That and the way he straightened in the chair and looked bolder convinced Slocum the pot was his for the taking. He could fold and give it to Stine or he could take it with his full house.

"You let me put in IOUs before. Will you again?"

"That's be for danged near a hundred dollars," Stine said. "A lot of money, but why not? You're an honest man."

This almost caused Slocum to back down, but greed got the better of him. He dropped his IOU into the pot and showed his full house.

"Sorry, John, but that's not good enough." Stine dropped four treys onto the table. "Now how are you going to pay me back?"

The direct gaze told Slocum he had been had. He said, "I suspect I'm going to find out."

Abel Stine grinned from ear to ear.

•   •   •

"Yes, sir," Stine said as they worked the pump on the handcar heading down the track in the Denver rail yard, "the minute I saw you cut down that cowboy I knew you were the man for the job."

Slocum's shoulders ached from the constant up and down pumping that kept the handcar moving. Stine seemed indefatigable, but Slocum wasn't used to work like this. Worse, he knew he had been a sucker back in the saloon, no better than a greenhorn from the way Stine had taken him.

"I'm not a hired gunman," Slocum declared.

"Don't want that. Want someone with your brains—and your fast hand. The railroad's been hit time and again, and we don't hardly know where the trouble's coming from," Stine said. "I've worked for Mr. Atkinson for well nigh eight years now, and I'd give my life for the man."

"I feel like I'm buying into that," Slocum said, swiping at the rivers of sweat pouring down his face. The hot Colorado summer sun sucked the juices from him as fast as if he'd been on foot in the middle of the Sonora Desert.

Stine laughed. "Mr. Atkinson is a good man to work for. He's a rarity among railroad magnates—an honest man. But he's up against some varmints who won't stop at anything, including murder, to keep him from building his road."

"Where is the site? Somewhere south of Santa Fe?" Slocum asked.

This produced a deep laugh from Abel Stine. "Not that far. We'll get out of Denver and pick up a supply train leaving from our supply depot. Go on to Pueblo and then south from there. We won't be pumping all the way to the canyon."

"Tell me about the Colorado and New Mexico railroad," Slocum said, hoping this would take his mind off the ache starting in his back and spreading throughout his body.

"Ever since the Union Pacific came in and Jay Gould got his sticky fingers on its control, the smaller roads have been in trouble. Gould's a sharp operator and not above driving out his competition with lower freight rates and . . ."

"And some violence?" asked Slocum.

"That's so," Stine admitted reluctantly. "The competition among the smaller railroads gets fiercer because of Gould. The only way to fight him is to get bigger. General Palmer's Denver and Rio Grande is like that. The General's pushing on out to Salt Lake City, as well as into the Rockies to get ore from the silver mines to the smelters."

"Where does Atkinson fit in?"

"Down south is some rugged terrain, deep canyons, and possibly rich gold and silver deposits. Cheap transport in for the miners and their supplies, cheap transport out for their ore and, well, that spells big profits."

"You think Gould's behind sabotaging your trestle and rails?"

Stine shook his head. "Can't blame him. Truth is, he might not even notice us yet, but there are others who have." Stine spat and then said, "Villalobos, now, he notices. He wants the same site where Atkinson is crossing Cutthroat Gorge. If he doesn't get it, he has to detour ten miles away at a harder crossing. That's a powerful lot of track to lay and bridge to build. The C and NM would be into the ore fields a month before he could arrive."

"There's the depot," Slocum said.

"You act like we been pumpin' this all day. It's only been twenty minutes," Stine said. He stepped back and let the handle go up and down a few times until the handcar came to a halt by a siding. Stine dropped off, threw the switch, and pushed the car down the track and off the main line.

"We *will* be riding in a train to Pueblo?" Slocum asked.

"You want to go up with the engineer and shovel coal? Old Jeffers can always use a second fireman."

"I want to ride. Don't even care if we have to sit on wood flooring, but I'm not inclined to want to stoke a furnace in this heat."

"We'll do better 'n that," Stine promised. He motioned for Slocum to follow him across the tracks. Rolling stock from a half dozen different narrow-gauge lines moved through the bustling rail yard. "I guarantee a ride in luxury since we'll be taking Mr. Atkinson's private engine. He's already south at the gorge and—"

Slocum reached out and caught the foreman's arm. He felt the heavy muscle there tense. Stine had seen the trouble brewing when he had.

"What do you want to do?" Slocum asked.

"There's only two of us. No tellin' how many of them there are," Stine said. "I'm not a coward and I'm not a quitter, but I do have the sense God gave a goose."

He backed away, and Slocum went with him. Between two freight cars stood a half dozen men, all armed with long ax handles. Not a one of them looked friendly enough to say howdy to. If Slocum and Stine had walked into that artificial canyon, they stood to get their heads pounded in.

"Who are they?"

"Might be Villalobos's men. Might be a gang hanging out in the yards," Stine said. "Doesn't much matter since either one'd leave the pair of us dead."

They hadn't gone twenty paces when another group of men blocked their retreat. Slocum looked around for a place to make a stand. He nudged Stine and said, "Down there. We can hole up in a car. That ought to give some protection to our backs."

"That's Villalobos's train," Stine warned.

"What's the difference?"

"He kills us there, he can claim to Atkinson—and the

law—we were trespassing. Or worse. He can claim we were out to steal from him."

"Can't see how that's worse." Slocum jumped into an empty car and looked around. Getting trapped inside would be deadly.

"It's a matter of honor. Mr. Atkinson has always said he never did anything underhanded to get ahead. Villa-lobos would love to show that's not so, just to disgrace him."

"I can think of things worse than people thinking Atkinson was a thief," Slocum said. He didn't add what that might be, but being dead came right at the top of the list. "Let's get to the top of the cars. We might jump across and get out that way."

"Risky," Stine said, already working his way up hand over hand on the iron-rung ladder at the end of the freight car.

"Get 'em, boys, kill 'em good!" went up the cry.

This lent energy to Slocum's climb. He spilled onto the top of the car only to find Stine already jumping to the next. Slocum got his feet under him. His cowboy boots weren't very good for this kind of running. The wood roof of the freight car was slippery and sloping. He had to be careful not to make a misstep and slide off to the ground. A dozen or more men ran parallel to the tracks now, following their loud progress atop the train.

Every step he and Stine took echoed in the empty cars and betrayed their location.

"Ahead, Slocum, there," Stine said. He bent over with his hands on his knees, winded. "That's where the Colorado and New Mexico cars are. Safety, if we can get there in one piece."

Behind them scrambled several of the toughs intent on bashing in their heads. And ahead in the engine stood a well-dressed man, his face in shadow, directing the chase.

"Jump!" Stine called, already in the air. He barely

reached the top of the car in the train alongside Villalobos's. Slocum followed more easily, but he fell to his
knees. Before he recovered, he heard the sharp command
from the direction of the engine.

"Kill them!"

A shot tore through the air next to Slocum's head. He
ducked involuntarily. As he went into a crouch, his hand
closed around his Colt Navy. He drew, located the man
shooting at him and fired three times. One of the rounds
knocked the man from the top of the other car. His attacker yelped in pain, dropped his gun, and flailed about
as he fell off.

This slowed their pursuers for only an instant. Others
opened up on them. Slocum fired three more times, emp-
tying his Colt.

"We've got to get out of here," he said, spinning around
and crashing into Stine and another man locked in a
deadly fight. The trio fell to the top of the freight car and
rolled over and over. The man held a rifle and discharged
it.

Stine yelled in pain, fingers burned on the metal barrel.
As he released his grip, the man he fought tried to get the
muzzle lowered and shoved into Stine's gut. Slocum
swung his six-gun and caught the man above the right
eye, sending him to the ground. Before the fallen man's
rifle slid off the car, Slocum dived onto it.

Levering in another round, he dropped onto his belly
and began firing. The first shot took the leg out from under a gunman. The second drove the remainder of their
assailants off the tops of the cars.

Slocum turned the rifle toward the engine, hoping for
a shot at the man directing the battle, but he was too late.
He saw the flash of a fancy brocade jacket, and then there
was only darkness there. For a moment.

His finger tightened and then relaxed when another figure came into view. Slocum didn't get much of a look at

her, but the woman was gorgeous. Then she followed the man off the engine and into hiding.

"Come on, Slocum," urged Stine. "We can't stay here, or they'll get us for sure."

Slocum followed the railroad foreman across the yards to the safety of Clarence Atkinson's warehouses.

2

"Are you still in one piece?" asked Stine, finally finding some sanctuary among the warehouses. He limped toward Slocum and then sank to the ground, sitting in the cinders. "That was a hell of a fight." Through it all, the man had kept on his knit cap. In the sun, during the gunfight, he had never let it slip off his head. Slocum shook his head in amazement.

"When I lost the poker hand I never thought paying off my debt would be this hard." Slocum dusted off his shirt and ignored his pants. They were stained with pitch from the freight car roof and so much dirt that even a hard scrubbing might not be enough to get them clean again.

"Knew you were the man for the job," Stine said, getting to his feet. "Mr. Atkinson is gonna appreciate havin' you on his side."

Slocum looked as if he had bitten into a sour persimmon. "Remind me how much money I need to work off."

"You'll get a bonus to make it worth your time, Slocum," Stine assured him. Slocum wasn't sure it would be enough.

"Who were those bushwhackers? I saw the owlhoot sending them out. He was well dressed, but I didn't get

13

a close look at his face." Slocum hesitated mentioning the lovely woman. She had appeared distraught, as if not approving of what happened in the rail yard but doing nothing to persuade the man that he ought to stop his dry-gulching ways.

"That'd be Carlos Villalobos's foreman, unless I miss my guess. Villalobos is a Mexican vaquero who took it into his head that railroads were better 'n cows. He sold his ranchero down Mexico way and moved north, buying railroads, and if he couldn't buy 'em, he built 'em. He saw how Mr. Atkinson was putting out feeder lines and decided that was his market, too."

"Did he try buying the Colorado and New Mexico?"

"Reckon so, but Mr. Atkinson wouldn't sell. Railroading is his life. Nothing will ever get him to sell out, less it means he can go build another 'road somewhere else."

Slocum grunted in disgust. A war over a railroad line seemed a damned fool thing to get involved in. Just as stupid as a bar fight.

"Come on and let's find the rest of the crew," Stine said, threading his way through the warehouses as if he were a cougar following a game trail. Slocum trailed, reloading his six-gun as he walked. By the time they reached the short train with its engine already under pressure and straining to hurl itself southward down the tracks, Slocum was loaded for bear again.

"These are some of the men I've already hired as guards," Stine said in way of introduction. Slocum only glanced at the half dozen men standing outside the fancy parlor car, some smoking, others bragging to one another. None of them had the look of a railroad worker. These men were stone killers.

And Slocum was one of them now. A guard. He snorted in disgust. He had to remember not to be suckered into poker games with men who faked their tells in the future.

Still, Slocum couldn't be too hard on himself. From all he had seen Abel Stine was a smart, tough hombre, even if he never took off the ridiculous knit cap.

"On board, gents. We're on our way to Pueblo and then on down to the spot where Mr. Atkinson is layin' track." Something about the way Stine spoke put Slocum on guard. The foreman was holding something back, but Slocum settled down into a well-padded seat and leaned back to enjoy the trip. He was bone-tired and needed some sleep. He tipped his black, floppy brimmed hat down over his eyes but didn't go to sleep. Instead, he listened to the talk ebbing and flowing around him.

Somewhere along the way Slocum did go to sleep, only to come awake with a start when the engine slowed.

"What's wrong?" he demanded of Stine. The foreman walked back down the aisle in the parlor car, rousing the sleepy men. Stine looked down at Slocum, his expression grim.

"We got a small project to finish off 'fore we get on farther down the line," Stine said.

"What is it?"

"Grab a rifle," Stine said, moving on. Slocum saw a crate of Winchesters open at the front of the car. Next to it lay an opened burlap bag filled with boxes of cartridges. Some of the men were already loading their rifles, not bothering to wonder what was being asked of them. Slocum swung out of the soft seat and took a second to get his balance. The train still puffed along at a decent clip, although it was slowing.

"What are we getting ourselves into?" Slocum asked the foreman again.

"You got a curiosity that'll get you killed, Slocum."

"I've done a good job staying alive by asking questions, and if I don't like the answers, I do something about it."

"All right," Stine said. Louder he called out to everyone, "Listen up. Slocum and I were shot at and almost killed back in the Denver rail yard. We're gonna get some revenge by slowing down one of Villalobos's shipments along his own line."

"You want us to pull out a rail or two?" asked one of the men. "Any train comin' along'll be derailed that way." He laughed harshly and added, "Might even kill a few of the bastards in the wreck."

"We are going to stop a shipment of rails Villalobos ordered. If we scatter them across the countryside, it'll put him days behind schedule. I don't much care if the train's damaged, either," Stine added. Everyone but Slocum joined in a raucous cheer at the idea of spilling blood.

Stine turned to Slocum and spoke in a low voice. "I know you don't cotton much to this, Slocum, but we need to do it. Villalobos is putting fearsome pressure on Mr. Atkinson. We've got to win some breathing room."

"All right," Slocum said, knowing he was making a mistake.

The train screeched to a halt, and they got off. In the distance to the north Slocum saw dark, billowing clouds from the Pueblo foundries turning out the steel rail needed to build a railroad. He settled his rifle in the crook of his left arm and started climbing a hill behind the others. Stine was already pointing out their target when he reached the summit.

"Down there," Stine said. "See that track? Narrow gauge, just like Mr. Atkinson lays, but this is Villalobos's line—the Colorado Southern. Take out a spike or two on a rail and the entire train derails. That's all we have to do, gents."

"I want to kill something," a burly man groused.

"You'll get your fill of fighting," Stine said. "Later, when we get to camp."

Slocum hung back some as the others rushed downhill and across a level area on the Colorado plateau to put their backs to pulling out spikes already driven by Villa-lobos's crew.

"This isn't something I can go along with," Slocum told the foreman. "I'll face any man trying to kill me, but sabotage?" He shook his head. "I saw too much of it during the war. It's cowardly. You have a problem, meet it head on."

"We can't," Stine said. "Villalobos has more men, has more money, has the upper hand no matter which way we turn."

"Then why doesn't he just ride into your camp and wipe you out?" asked Slocum.

"He's a sneaky bastard, that's why. Besides, it's cheaper to potshot us one at a time. Being in camp is like being a target. That's why you and them boys are going to be so important. Keep Villalobos's snipers from killing or wounding our workers, and we'll beat him every time."

"But this?"

Stine smiled without any humor. "It's along the way and an easy way of getting back at him."

Slocum turned when he heard the steel rails whining.

"Train's coming!" he called to the others.

"We got them spikes pulled out. We kin lift the rail out of place and—"

"Get off the tracks," Stine ordered. "We've done all we can. Now—"

The freight train chugging along put on its brakes and set yard-long orange and yellow sparks flaring from its wheels. The train had not been going fast enough to carry it through the sabotaged section of track. Instead, a dozen armed men jumped from the train and opened fire.

Slocum put the rifle butt to his shoulder and squeezed off a round. The slug went wide but sent the intended target to the ground hunting for cover. That was good enough for Slocum. For the moment. He swung his rifle around and found another possible target. Then he was the one dodging slugs and hunting for cover.

The bullets winging their way up from the train were joined by others from uphill, in the direction of the Atkinson train and tracks.

"Stine, what's going on?" shouted Slocum. "Are those our own men shooting at us?"

"It's a trap," Stine called back. "They got us in a cross fire."

Slocum looked around and saw little they could use for cover. He turned and started firing methodically, accurately, with deadly efficiency at the men above them on the hill. He winged one and killed another. But there had to be four or five left, all intent on ventilating him. Slocum finally dropped into a shallow ditch and wallowed in the mud to get down even lower.

A bullet ripped through the brim of his hat. He had to reload his rifle. Of all the men, he was the only one who had dropped a full box of cartridges into his pocket. He slid the last of six rounds he had fumbled out into his magazine, then passed the box to Stine, who doled out the rest to the others.

"Hold your fire until you've got a decent shot," Slocum said.

"Do as he says, men. He knows what he's doing," seconded Stine. "Save your ammo, if we need to shoot our way out."

Without telling the foreman what he intended, Slocum pulled himself out of the muddy ditch and ran in a crouch, dodging bullets as he went. He ran between the two groups firing at them, getting Villalobos's train to his back and the others uphill firing at his face. Then he opened up, firing first in one direction and then in the other.

When all six rounds were spent, Slocum went to ground again. The air above him filled with lead flying in both directions. Wiggling like a snake, Slocum made it back to where Stine and the others watched the fight in wonder.

"You got them shooting at each other. That's real smart, Slocum, real smart."

"We can't stay here. Too exposed," Slocum said. He grabbed one man by the collar and pulled him over. "How far did you get pulling out the spikes?"

"Got 'em out all the way," the man said proudly. Slocum cursed. He had intended to hijack the train and ride it to safety. There had to be some other way to save their hides.

Already the men from the train were calling to the others to stop firing. It would be only seconds before both groups turned back to shooting at Stine and his men.

"We run for it," Slocum said. "Along the tracks. That way, away from the train."

"They'll come after us," protested the man who had been so proud of yanking out the spikes.

"Good," Slocum said. Not waiting to argue, he bolted for the tracks and ran like a rabbit between the ties. Then Slocum jumped to the far side and kept running the best he could as bullets sought to kill him. Head down and arms pumping, he ran like the wind. From behind he heard the huffing and puffing of the men Stine had hired. They didn't know what was going on, but staying behind to get shot up didn't appeal to any of them.

"Cain't say I like runnin' like a coward," a burly man growled from behind Slocum.

"Keep running," Slocum ordered. He wondered where Stine was. He liked the curious railroad foreman, knit cap and all, and would be sorry to see him killed. If Stine died in this trap, Slocum would never go on into Clarence Atkinson's camp. He'd have no reason to.

"They can't keep up with us," gasped the man, already slowing. "They're comin' after us in the train!"

Slocum pulled up and turned to see that the man was right. Stine crashed into him and almost knocked him over. He pushed Stine aside and drew his six-shooter, getting off a couple quick shots in the direction of the men chasing them.

"Fire, shoot them!" Slocum cried. He heard a bullet ricochet off the front of the engine. And then huge plumes of white steam gusted upward from the train as it began moving sluggishly forward. The bushwhackers who had been shooting at them all jumped aboard the train, hoping to chase them down. They had not realized how close they had come to the sabotaged section of track—if they had anticipated such treachery at all.

"The rails," gloated Stine. "The train's going over the loosened rails!"

"Good," Slocum said without emotion. He had not been in favor of this, but then the tables had turned. Better for Villalobos's men to die than for him to end up in some potter's field.

Even as the foreman spoke, the train slid onto the sabotaged rail. It twisted up under the train, sending out sparks and ear-splitting noise. Then the engine leaned slightly to the left. The pitch grew and the train toppled like some behemoth falling from a great height. With it went the cars it pulled, both the passenger car loaded with guards and the flatcars carrying steel rail.

"We did it, we did it!" cried Stine, dancing a little jig.

Slocum watched the engine sliding on its side. Men screeched in agony and death, and the ones left uphill melted away like fog in the hot morning sun. Then the earth shook as the boiler exploded, sending metal fragments in all directions like some oversized mine.

"We did what you wanted," Slocum said coldly to the foreman. "Let's get to the construction site."

Stine glared at Slocum, not approving of his attitude but unable to say anything. It had been Slocum who had saved them. They hiked over the hill and down the far side to where their engine puffed impatiently, waiting for them to return. In ten minutes they were heading south away from Pueblo and toward the steep canyon country where Clarence Atkinson sought to build a spur to the Colorado and New Mexico railroad.

"I can pick 'em," Stine said, settling beside Slocum in the padded seat. "You took over when we needed you most. You must have been an officer during the war."

"Villalobos won't let you get away with destroying an engine and killing that many men. To hell with getting behind schedule. He'll come after you with blood in his eye."

"It's nothing we haven't put up with before. Railroading's a tough occupation, Slocum. If Villalobos hadn't started it, if he had just tried to finish his tracks before us, there wouldn't be this kind of bad blood. As long as he tries to kill us rather than deal, what choice do we have?"

"I don't know," Slocum said. "How long before we get to the C and NM work site?"

"Ten hours. We got some pretty country to ride through first."

"You ride a horse," Slocum said. "I'm not sure what you do on a train speeding along at twenty miles an hour."

Stine laughed and slapped Slocum on the shoulder. "You sound like a cowboy, but you know about trains. Won't be long 'fore I'm worryin' you'll be after my job." With that Stine pulled down his knit cap and went to talk with the others. From somewhere they had found a bottle of whiskey and were celebrating their victory. Slocum let them drink. He had an uneasy feeling something wasn't quite right.

He tried to sleep but the feeling grew. He got up and went to the car end of the parlor car and opened the door leading back to the freight cars they pulled. He went onto the small platform and looked out one side and then the other. The country had turned more mountainous, as Stine had promised, and deep canyons stretched away from the tracks.

Slocum leaned out and peered up, wondering if any of Villalobos's men had climbed onto their train. He didn't know where the second bunch of bushwhackers had come from and why they hadn't seen the train. Maybe they had been too intent on catching themselves some of Atkinson's men. Take the raiding party prisoner, then go after Atkinson's train.

Slocum nodded. That was the way he would have done it. But he would also have left a man or two on guard. Climbing a steel rung ladder, he got to the top of the train and looked the entire length. This time the freight cars were filled with nothing but supplies for the men: food, blankets, spare clothing. Another train would bring along the hardware required to keep the tracks being laid.

Turning, Slocum faced forward. The wind dried his face and forced him to squint. The sun was going down in the west, casting long shadows across the land. They had entered the mountains some time back and rattled over one small bridge after another. Ahead loomed a notch blasted through the mountain. The silver threads of railroad track went into the notch, making it appear as if Slocum were sighting down a rifle barrel and past the front gun sight.

He dropped back down to the platform and went into the parlor car. The men who weren't passed out were swapping lies about how brave they had been during the skirmish. Even Stine was three sheets to the wind.

Going forward, Slocum left the parlor car and edged along the coal tender to the engine. A fireman, stripped to the waist, worked tirelessly to stoke the boiler. The engineer hung out the side, intent on something ahead.

Slocum's sixth sense had kept him alive during the war and after. He was not going to deny its message now.

"Anything wrong?" he shouted to the engineer. The

man pulled his head back, frowned and shrugged.

"Can't say. We're getting to the top of the pass. The bridge on the far side goes over the river. It's always been a tad rickety, so I'm slowin' down for it."

Going over a weak bridge wasn't something Slocum needed to hear about, but it made him feel a bit better. That was what he had worried over without knowing the cause.

"Any danger?"

" 'Course there is, but I made it a dozen times this month already without any problem. I know how to drive this iron-bellied beast, mister. Get on back to your fancy-ass car and live it up and let me do my work. Oh, holy hell!"

The engineer grabbed a cord and pulled it hard, braking the engine. He pulled on levers and struggled to stop the train.

"What's wrong?" asked Slocum. Like an echo came the same question from a frightened-sober Abel Stine.

"Lookee there," the engineer said. "Good thing we made such good time. If I'd hit this bridge in the dark an hour later I'd never have seen that barricade."

Ahead, across the tracks were a dozen railroad ties. From what Slocum could see, they had been fastened to the tracks with wire. A train hitting them at any speed would have been derailed and sent plunging into the hundred-foot gorge.

He leaned out and stared down at the river, a tributary to the San Juan, he guessed. It was a long way down into the cold water. Slocum shivered, realizing how close they had come to disaster.

"I see what you mean, Stine," he said. "This isn't business competition. It's outright war."

"No prisoners taken," Stine added. "Come on, Slocum. The rest of them are sleeping off their drunk. We can get those ties shoved off and be in camp before midnight."

Slocum walked carefully along the tracks, wary that a single misstep would send him plunging through the bridge ties down to the river. The barricade had been erected only a few yards out from the safety of track laid on bedrock.

Slocum scratched his head as he stared at the obstruction.

"What's wrong?" asked Stine. "Get a move on and help me."

"Why'd they put the barricade here?" he asked. "It's almost as if they wanted us to see it and stop with the train entirely on the bridge."

"What are you getting at?"

The explosion from under the train blew out the center trestle supports. Slocum saw the engine begin its downward fall, as if dipped in molasses, and then a second explosion picked him up gently only to crush his body with brutal force a split second later.

3

Blood. Blood running down his arms. John Slocum fought to understand what was going on. He tasted dust in his mouth, mingled with blood. And his eyes. He was blind. He panicked and clawed at the rock under his fingers, then realized the cause of his blindness. Blood. It was the curious, entirely black curtain of blood trickling into his eyes. Forcing himself to calm, he blinked rapidly.

Slowly, light came back and with it a blurred view of the world. The shock of the explosion wore off gradually, and he remembered what had happened.

"Stine, where are you?" He remembered the foreman standing next to him when the trestle blew to hell and gone. "Are you all right?"

"Slocum?" came the weak reply. "I hurt all over my damn body."

Slocum didn't bother answering. He ached, too. Vision returned gradually as he wiped repeatedly his forehead to keep more of the blood from blinding him. His clothes were tattered and burned, and he didn't bother counting the number of minor cuts all over his back. But major injury had passed him by this time. On shaky legs he walked from the still-intact barricade to the edge of the bridge and looked down.

The shock of seeing the steel rails cut off as clean as a sharp knife slicing through cheese stopped him for a moment. Then he looked beyond the abrupt end of the track. Most of the bridge, along with the engine and cars, had tumbled to the river below. The twisted, broken look of the heavy engine told him no one had survived that fall.

"They got 'em all," Stine said, coming up beside him and staring down into the gorge. "The sons of bitches!"

"Who?" asked Slocum.

"Villalobos and his hired killers, who else? Who else has any reason to murder my men like this?"

"You said Jay Gould was moving into the state," Slocum said. "Might be he wants to scare Clarence Atkinson into selling."

"This won't scare Mr. Atkinson. It'll only put lead in his pencil and make him all the more determined."

Slocum brushed himself off and backed from the edge of the precipice. The barricade was still held over the tracks by heavy wire. Slocum climbed to the top and looked around, not seeing much more than he had from the ground. The notch in the mountain ahead deprived him of any option other than hiking along the tracks. He sure as hell couldn't go back across the gorge.

"It'll take two weeks to rebuild this bridge. We need this line to supply our camp," grumbled Stine.

"How many men got themselves killed?" Slocum asked.

"The engineer and fireman and, well, the guards I hired. We were lucky. No conductor on that train." The way he dismissed the guards he had hired told Slocum Abel Stine was a complete railroader and had nothing but disdain for anyone not working to lay track. That put his own position in its proper place. Any obligation due Stine—and it had been nothing more than money owed for a bet gone bad—was past.

"Unless you have some reason to sit and spit into the

canyon, let's start walking," Slocum said. He jumped to the far side of the barrier and trudged uphill, cinders crunching under his boots with every step. With each step Slocum grew more furious. Shooting a man in a fight was one thing, planting a bomb and killing him by blowing a bridge out from under him was something else. There was killing . . . and there was cowardly murder.

Slocum wanted to get even with the man who had done this.

"You fixin' on leavin', Slocum?" asked Stine. "There's no reason for you to stay. Whatever you owe me from the poker game is a forgiven debt."

"I'll stay," Slocum said. He had gone from hot anger to a cold fury at Villalobos—or whoever had planted the bomb.

"Thanks. I reckon we're gonna need men like you. Not like the others, rest their souls. They were killers because they enjoyed killing. I was wrong hiring them."

"How far is the construction camp?" Slocum didn't want the foreman to get too maudlin over the deaths of men he considered backshooters and worse.

Stine started to answer, then dropped to his knees and bent over, pressing his ear to the rails. Slocum put his foot on the rail and felt the vibration caused by the distant, powerful locomotive rumbling toward them.

"We'd better find a place and flag them down," Slocum said. "We don't want this engine going over the edge into the canyon, too."

"That's got to be Mr. Atkinson's private train," Stine said. "It's the only engine on this side of the bridge—or what's left of it. He wouldn't be coming if he didn't think something was mighty wrong."

They got to the top of a rise and saw the train chugging toward them, struggling up the steep slope. Abel Stine began waving furiously. Slocum took out his six-shooter in case he needed to fire a warning round or two. The

engineer was alert and spotted them in time to bring the
locomotive to a halt not twenty feet away. Stine hurried
over and climbed into the cab. Slocum trailed the foreman, wanting to look over the situation before getting too
involved.

Whatever happened, he would have to ride out on this
train unless he wanted to walk a powerful long ways.

"We got a ways to go back down the tracks," Stine
said, jumping to the ground from the engine cab. "The
train don't reverse too good, but it'll get us back to the
camp."

"If Atkinson was expecting the train we were on, he
intended to spend some time running backward," Slocum
pointed out.

"He came out after us. There was something that put a
bee in his bonnet. At least, that's what old Irish up there
in the engine said."

Slocum saw the engineer push his striped cap back on
his head, revealing a shock of bright red hair. There
wasn't much guesswork about how the engineer had come
by his nickname.

"Where do we sit?" asked Slocum. "My feet are mighty
sore."

He looked the length of the train and saw only the
engine, tender, and three cars, all of which looked like
fabulous gemstones on wheels. Beveled glass windows,
fancy woodwork, and what looked to be inlaid gold and
gilt around the doors told Slocum this wasn't a train de-
signed to carry freight.

The men and women who rode this train were special.

"Mr. Atkinson wants to talk to us personally," Stine
said. "Come on, Slocum. First car." The foreman caught
the ornate iron railing and pulled himself up. Slocum followed, eyeing the stained glass window in the small door
leading into the car. Stine rapped once and was greeted
with an immediate grunt from within.

"He's waiting for us," Slocum said sarcastically. Stine missed the tone, intent only on seeing his boss. The small door opened on well-oiled hinges.

"Mr. Atkinson," Stine said, touching a spot just above his eyebrow as if he were a private saluting his general. Slocum saw the foreman made no move to take off his knit cap. Slocum removed his own hat in deference to the man who owned the Colorado and New Mexico railroad.

Clarence Atkinson sat on a wooden chair that reminded Slocum of a throne used by English royalty he had seen in a book. Ornately carved, with arms that came out to end in silver-chased patterns, the chair dominated the room from its slight dais. Or it would have if the man sitting in it had not been of such overwhelming presence. Atkinson had a fringe of gray hair that floated over his ears like some kind of halo. A sharp, aquiline nose separated two piercing blue eyes set in a weathered face. His thin lips might have been cruel on occasion, but now were curled upward in a slight smile that seemed genuine.

"Abel!" the railroad magnate greeted. He shot to his feet, stepped off the dais and clutched Stine's hand, pumping it like the handle on a handcar. "I'm so glad you're safe. I heard rumors that Villalobos was going to try something underhanded and came to see if I could be of assistance."

"He blew the bridge out from under us," Stine said, his voice choked with emotion. "It's bad enough to destroy our property, but Villalobos tried to kill us."

"How many engines do you have?" asked Slocum.

"The one in the gorge and this one," Stine answered, his attention pulled from Atkinson. "Why?"

"Looks to be a good way of crippling your road," Slocum said. "Killing the men was incidental to slowing your progress."

"He's right," Atkinson said. "We can't bring in more supplies until the bridge is rebuilt. And I need to get my train across on the tracks and back to Denver. Denver's where the money is, after all. The mother's milk of any venture like this."

"I suppose buying a new engine is out of the question," Slocum said. "Might be possible to borrow one—or rent it—from some other road."

"A good idea," said Atkinson, stroking his clean-shaven chin. "You are a clever man."

"Oh," said Stine, embarrassed. "This is John Slocum. I hired him in Denver to be a guard."

"Brains as well as marksmanship, eh?" Atkinson eyed Slocum as if he were a side of beef. Slocum didn't flinch as the railroad magnate came to some unfathomable conclusion, then sat back down in his thronelike chair. Atkinson tented his fingers under his chin and peered over them at Stine and Slocum.

"We can take half the crew and get to work on the other bridge. Are you still blasting for the foundations of the trestle over Cutthroat Gorge?" Stine asked.

"There is a chance we can keep the entire crew busy, half rebuilding the destroyed bridge and the other putting in foundations for the new one," Atkinson said, thinking hard. "You know how to do it, Abel. You're a capable man, the best foreman I ever had."

"Thank you, sir, but I'm not feelin' too smart right about now. Not after losing an entire engine like that."

"It was a trap," Slocum cut in, "that nobody could have avoided. There was a barricade that would have derailed the train if the engineer had tried bulling his way through it. Either way, the train would have ended up in the bottom of that canyon."

"Yes, I'm sure Abel did his best," Atkinson said, irritated now. Slocum watched the storm cloud of anger rising on the man's face and saw the sheer power in him. His hands gripped the arms of his chair, and he said in a fiery voice, "This is war. I will not permit Villalobos to stop the C and NM Railroad!"

Slocum turned when the door at the rear of the car opened. In walked a lovely, well-dressed brunette woman. Slocum drank in her beauty and wondered where he had seen her before. She was middle-aged but still possessed a radiant, youthful beauty that appealed to Slocum. She turned slightly and allowed a younger woman, probably her daughter, to enter. Then Slocum knew why the older woman looked so familiar.

Her daughter was the woman he had seen in the Denver rail yard with Villalobos's foreman.

"Ah, my dear, come in," Atkinson said. "Allow me to introduce my wife, Henrietta. And behind her, acting unusually coy, is our daughter, Esther."

"Ladies," Slocum said. His eyes locked with Atkinson's daughter's, making her increasingly uneasy.

"Abel, you say your new friend is dependable and good with his gun?"

"Slocum, sir," Stine said. "I'd trust him with my life. He's saved it often enough on the way here, after all."

"That's recommendation enough for me. Slocum, you will guard my wife and daughter and keep them from harm. I have every reason to believe this will get more violent, and Villalobos might come after my family. Now, get on into the next car with you. Abel and I have some difficult decisions to make if we are to stay on schedule."

"Dear, I—" Henrietta Atkinson began.

"I said I had business," Clarence Atkinson coldly cut her off. "Save your undoubtedly petty concerns for later. Take Slocum into your car and give him tea or something."

"But, Clarence, I—"

Slocum saw the look between husband and wife and knew there was little love here. Atkinson was totally involved in building the railroad and had no time for anything trivial—such as his wife's obvious apprehension.

Without a word, Slocum walked the length of the car
and held the door for the women. Esther shied away from
him guiltily, then scurried like a rabbit through the door
into the next car. Slocum looked back. Atkinson and Stine
already had buried themselves in the details of building
two bridges at the same time: one repair, the other new
across Cutthroat Gorge.

"Ma'am," Slocum said, holding the door for Henrietta
Atkinson. She sniffed and bustled through. Slocum caught
the scent of her perfume. The odor of violets made him
momentarily dizzy with memories of spring in his old
homestead in Calhoun, Georgia. The rush of air between
the cars as the train worked its way backward down the
track had cleared his head by the time he entered the next
car.

"I don't know what you're supposed to do for us," Henrietta said, still distraught.

"Watch over you. It sounds like your husband's declared total war on a railroad rival."

"Carlos Villalobos?" Henrietta said with some disdain.
"What a terrible man. He deserves anything he gets. Now,
if you will excuse me, I want to lie down."

"Mother, please, don't go," Esther said, looking in
panic from Slocum to Henrietta and then back.

"I must, my dear. You and Mr. Slocum can figure out
exactly what it is your father wants him to do. Excuse
me, sir." With that Henrietta Atkinson went into the last
car.

Esther moved to a corner of the car, as if Slocum might
attack her.

"I'm here to protect you, Miss Atkinson," Slocum said,
"but I need to know what I'm protecting you from."

"I don't understand."

"I think you do. Back in Denver—" He never got any
further. The young woman ran to him and covered his

mouth with her cool fingers. Her breasts crushed against his chest, and her nearness sparked responses in Slocum he had not considered possible just a few seconds earlier. This was the daughter of his employer—and both parents were in adjoining cars.

"I'll make it worth your while never to say a word about seeing me there with Dunne," Esther whispered. She removed her hand and stared up, her brown eyes soft and dewy and her body promising Slocum paradise.

"That's not my job," he said.

"Your job's to keep me happy, isn't it?" she asked, her hand snaking down between them and finding his crotch. She squeezed suggestively. Slocum responded, hating himself for doing it.

"This isn't what your father hired me for," he said.

"But it's what I *want*," she countered. Esther's clever fingers worked off his gun belt and let it drop to the floor of the fancy parlor car. She quickly unbuttoned his jeans. She let out a tiny gasp of pleasure when he snapped out of the denim prison, ready for action. Esther ran her fingers up and down his length a few times, then lightly kissed the tip.

The tremor that went through Slocum felt more like a full-fledged earthquake. He knew this was wrong but couldn't stop himself. Try as he might to lie and tell himself he needed to find out more about Esther and Villalobos, it all came down to her being so seductively lovely.

Their lips met in a fierce, passionate kiss. All the emotions Slocum had been letting build up since Little Ben's death came rushing out. And Esther returned them doubled and tripled. Esther's full, red lips parted slightly and her tongue shot out to tickle and tease his. Then they played an oral hide-and-seek, tongues flashing from one mouth to another until Slocum felt as if he had just drunk an entire bottle of tarantula juice. He was wobbling on his feet.

Especially when she reached down and squeezed hard on him again.

"More," she whispered hotly in his ear before nibbling on it. "Give me more." Her slender leg rose and curled around his waist, pulling him in. Slocum made an amazing discovery. Under the layers of dress and petticoats Esther wasn't wearing any bloomers. His manhood slipped and slid in a moist promised land until Esther rose on tiptoe and positioned it perfectly.

Then she simply relaxed and sent him sailing deep up into her most intimate recess. They both gasped in mutual pleasure. She tightened her leg around his waist, pulled herself even more firmly into his crotch and began moving in a broad circular motion, slowly at first, then with greater need and insistence. His arms circled her waist and held her close as they moved together in the erotic dance.

Then Esther gasped out loud enough to awaken the dead. Slocum tried to stifle her outcry with a kiss, but she turned from him, panting and moaning as her desires ran wild. Before he could try to quiet her with some other tactic, he felt her inner muscles gripping him.

He lost all control then, rocking and swaying in a carnal embrace until he was spent.

She gasped and shivered, then lowered her leg. On shaky knees, Esther stepped away from him. She chastely pulled her skirts down and smiled wickedly.

"You are a man of *many* talents, Mr. Slocum." She eyed him hungrily. How she could have any sexual energy left after their brief, intense lovemaking was beyond Slocum.

"Looks to me as if you were doing it all," he answered. He hastily buttoned himself up and fastened his gun belt around his waist.

"All business so soon?" Esther taunted. "It's that way with all the men I meet." She looked around as if worried again about being overheard. "You won't tell Father, will you?"

"About this?" Slocum asked in astonishment.

"No, silly, not about us. About seeing me with Dunne."

Slocum shook his head in wonder. She had given him such intense pleasure and all to keep her liaison with Villalobos's foreman a secret. But from whom? Her mother or her father? Or both?

"Good. I knew you were an honorable gentleman from the minute I laid eyes—and other things—on you. You are a southerner, aren't you? Georgia would be my guess, from your accent. I once—"

Esther's rambling words were cut off by the train lurching to a sudden halt. Esther and Slocum fell into each other's arms, then parted quickly, as if the other had turned to molten fire. Gunshots forced Slocum into action. Slocum drew his Colt Navy and ran for the rear car, only to find himself target for a half dozen bullets.

4

Slocum fell back into the car, trying to avoid the bullets sailing past him. He blundered into Esther Atkinson, who let out a screech of surprise and fear as one of the bullets took off part of her elaborate hairdo.

"Stay down," Slocum said, taking his own advice. He dropped flat to the floor and wiggled like a snake to the narrow walkway between the cars. The door leading into Henrietta Atkinson's car had been riddled with bullets and looked like a screen door. Slocum pulled the door open a fraction and peered past, hoping the shooters were still inside. He saw no movement and acted instantly.

It was foolhardy, but he had no choice. He threw open the door and thrust his six-shooter into the room, swaying back and forth like the head of an angry rattler. Getting to his feet, he went into the ornately appointed car, past the armoire and to the bed, using it as a shield. The back door stood open, pulled from its hinges. That told Slocum more than he could find out searching every square inch of the parlor car for some sign as to who had kidnapped Henrietta.

He made his way to the door and peered out into the mountainous region where the train had stopped. At first he couldn't figure out what was wrong. Then Slocum noticed how the car canted slightly to one side. Someone had put a railroad tie on the tracks and derailed the car. This had caused the entire train to come to a halt—and it had let the kidnappers enter Henrietta's car.

Swinging out onto the back platform, Slocum looked around, trying to find some hint of where the men might have gone. They would not be moving very fast dragging an unwilling woman along with them. Even if Henrietta Atkinson was terrified, she would put up some struggle and slow the retreat.

That was what he had hoped, but Slocum didn't find it. It was as if the men—and Clarence Atkinson's wife—had vanished into thin air.

"What's going on?" demanded Esther, coming up behind him. She pressed close, that body that he had possessed so delightfully only a few minutes earlier. Now Esther's trim body trembled with fear as she clung to his arm. He wanted to brush her off and get on the trail of the men who had taken her mother, but he found himself hesitating. He didn't want to be that abrupt with her.

"Go find your father or Abel Stine," he told her. "You'll be safe with them. I have to earn my keep." He held up the six-gun so she could see it and get the message. Esther's brown eyes grew wide, and she covered her mouth with her fingertips.

"Oh, no. This is serious, isn't it?"

Slocum was dumbfounded at that. They had been shot at and almost killed by their attackers. How could anyone miss that, even a sheltered, hothouse flower like Esther Atkinson?

"This isn't some lark," he told her. "Your father's business enemies aren't going to stop at killing a few of his hired hands. They're going after his family now."

"Mother's been—?" Esther seemed incapable of understanding the gravity of the situation.

"Go on, find your father and have him look after you," Slocum said, vaulting over the gilded iron platform railing. He hit the ground hard and stayed in a crouch. Glancing back, he saw he was right. The car had been derailed. The splinters under the parlor car might have been from a ruined railroad tie but he couldn't tell and that didn't matter. Finding Henrietta was his focus now.

Looking at the ground yielded no clues. The rocky area on either side of the railroad bed wasn't going to take a footprint unless a locomotive ran over it. Slocum mentally relived the attack, where the bullets trying to ventilate him had come from, the angles, everything. He turned to his right and dropped into an arroyo running parallel to the tracks.

He smiled when he saw the trampled prickly pear cluster and other signs men had passed by recently. Then the smile faded. He had to find which way they had gone, back in the direction of the destroyed bridge or toward the Colorado and New Mexico camp.

"Back," he decided. Whoever had planted the bomb on the bridge trestle might have waited to see the results of his handiwork. There might be even more of Villalobos's men—or whoever had taken Henrietta—lurking. If things were as dire as Atkinson hinted, Villalobos might launch an all-out attack on the C&NM camp, starting with an innocent woman.

Slocum's grip tightened on the ebony handle of his Colt Navy as he stalked along, wanting to run flat out and knowing he would only alert the kidnappers or blunder into a trap. Either way, he died—and so did Henrietta.

"Slocum!" came the shout from the direction of the train. Slocum recognized Stine's voice. "Where are you? Get on back here right away!"

Slocum kept moving. The foreman probably wanted to give orders, ones Slocum was following *before* they were given. He'd get Henrietta Atkinson back safe and sound.

If it took killing every bushwhacker in Villalobos's employ, so be it. He was tired of being the target, along with innocent women.

The arroyo branched. Slocum fell to his knees and looked at the rocky, sandy bottom. Faint imprints showed men had gone up the branch. Slocum hurried now, feeling an urgency. He thought Henrietta would be used as a poker chip in this high-stakes game, but he didn't doubt for a minute that neither side would bluff. From what he had seen of Clarence Atkinson, the man might just let his wife die rather than surrender his railroad.

"Now?" came the faint sound from ahead. "Can we kill her now?"

"Not yet. You know what the boss wanted."

"What's the meaning of this?" Henrietta Atkinson said in a clear, sharp voice. There was no hint of fear in her words, and Slocum worried that there ought to be. These men intended to kill her. Like her daughter, Henrietta was oblivious to the world around her and the dangers in it. He wondered if she had even gone along willingly with the men, seeing no reason to protest.

Slocum climbed from the wash and kept low to keep from being seen before he located the kidnappers. He paused and turned slowly, listening hard. The wind whistled down from the mountains and here and there stirred small animals, intent on nothing more than feeding. A rustle of fabric told Slocum where to look. He kept climbing until he got to the top of a rise and peered down. Henrietta faced a man with a long pink scar running across his face.

"You let me go now!" she demanded. He shoved her to the ground. The expression on her face was total surprise. No one treated the wife of a railroad magnate like this!

"I'm gonna use you, then I'm gonna kill you," the man said. "What do you think about that?"

Henrietta sputtered, but the other man only laughed and said, "I think she'll like it, Pete, getting a real man for a change. That husband of hers has got to be—"

"You shut your filthy mouth!" Henrietta raged, gathering her skirts about her and trying to get up. The man she had accosted shoved her back. The instant he tucked his gun into his belt to free his hands so he could rip off her clothing, Slocum aimed and fired. The bullet entered the back of the man's head and blasted out the face, spattering blood and gore all over Henrietta.

She was shocked, but the dead man's partner was paralyzed with fear. That gave Slocum time to cock his Colt again, swing the muzzle slightly and sight in on the other kidnapper. This time his shot went wide. He only blew off the man's ear.

"Yeow!" the man shrieked, clutching his head in pain. This was the last thing he did, the last thought he had, the last pain he felt. Slocum's next slug ripped out his foul heart.

Sliding down the slope Slocum got to his feet in front of Henrietta. He reached out to offer her a hand up. She glared at him and got to her feet herself.

"You ruined my dress. Look at this! Blood *never* comes out, and I had this special ordered from Denver."

It was Slocum's turn to be shocked. Henrietta was more outraged at ruining her dress than she was at the two sudden, violent deaths.

"They were going to . . . kill you," he said in growing wonder. The men had threatened more than simple death, and the woman knew it. Slocum saw no way of politely pointing this out to her.

"They won't be anything but buzzard bait now," she said in disgust. "Who did they work for? Do you think Carlos Villalobos actually hired them to kidnap me?"

"That's sure to put pressure on your husband," Slocum pointed out.

"I suppose," she said in resignation. "It gets so hard dealing with everyone my husband crosses."

"We'd better get back to the train. Mr. Atkinson must be worried about you."

Slocum almost expected another harsh laugh at his observation. After seeing her turn all meek and mild when Clarence Atkinson had ordered her from his railroad car, he had thought Henrietta was a mousy woman who had married above her station. Now he wasn't so certain. She had an iron core that appealed to him.

"I've been feeling so ill lately," Henrietta said, hiking alongside him, "I let those bullies break in. They caught me napping, in many senses of the word."

"What would you have done if you hadn't been feeling poorly?" Slocum had to ask. The answer did not surprise him at all now.

"I'd have shot them. And I would have made sure they didn't bleed all over my expensive dress." She rubbed at the blood on the front of her skirt, then snorted in disgust. "The stain is permanent. It'll never come out."

"And those men will never draw another breath," Slocum said.

"You are a good shot. Clarence did well hiring you. Or was it Abel? Yes, definitely Abel. Clarence would never know where to find a man like you."

"What kind of man would he hire?" Slocum asked, curious now.

"Ones like those you left dead," she said, disdain in her tone. "He can be a complete fool at times. At most times." She staggered and Slocum caught her. Henrietta was pale and sweat beaded her forehead. She hung limp as a dishrag in his arms. He lowered her to the ground.

"Are you all right?" he asked, brushing her sweat-sticky hair from her forehead. "You're burning up with fever."

"It's not so bad," she lied. "Give me a minute. Then we can return."

"Have you seen a doctor? You ought to be in Denver where one can look after you. This might be serious."

"I'm taking medicine," she said, small dollops of color returning to her pale cheeks. "Perhaps I ought to take some more of it. It's back in my car."

Slocum scooped her up in his arms. She was quite an armful. She threw her arms around his neck and put her head down on his shoulder. For a moment Slocum worried she might have died. Then he felt the slow, even gusts of the woman's warm breath on his neck. She wasn't dead; she was asleep, tuckered out from her ordeal.

Working his way up out of the arroyo, he got back to the railroad tracks and walked down toward the engine. The engineer—the one Stine had called Old Irish—waved to him, then turned and shouted for Abel Stine and Clarence Atkinson. The two men came boiling out of the railroad owner's car.

"Is she all right, Slocum?" asked Stine.

"She's not dead, is she? Stupid bitch was always . . ." Atkinson's voice trailed off when he saw Henrietta stir and her brown eyes blink open. "My dear Henrietta!" he cried, changing his tone entirely. "Let me have her, Slocum. You've done enough damage for one day. Give her to me!"

Slocum gently passed the stirring woman to her husband's arms, but Clarence Atkinson dropped her legs, supporting her around the shoulders only. Henrietta's legs buckled a little, but she strengthened.

"She said something about medicine in her car," Slocum said.

"Of course, of course," Atkinson said. "This way, my dear." He almost dragged Henrietta after him.

"What a loving husband," Slocum said under his breath. He wasn't sure Abel Stine heard. If he had, he might have been angry. Louder, Slocum asked, "What'd he mean by that crack I'd done enough damage? I got her back before the kidnappers raped her."

"What?" Stine's eyes went wide. "I didn't mean Mrs. Atkinson. I meant—" Stine clamped his mouth shut when Atkinson bellowed.

"They took my daughter, Slocum! You let them kidnap my daughter from under your nose!"

Slocum stood stock-still, not sure what to say. Esther had been safe in her car when the two outlaws had dragged off Henrietta Atkinson. He had told her to find Stine or her father for safety. Something had happened between the time Slocum had gone to rescue her mother and Esther had reached the front of the train.

Slocum's mind raced as he went over the possibilities. He didn't like any of the conclusions he reached. Either a second band of owlhoots had lain in wait for Esther and had not revealed themselves until he was gone, or she had gone willingly.

Why the hell was Dunne with Esther in the Denver rail yard?

"Get in, Slocum," said Stine. "We jacked the train and got the wheels back on the tracks. It's a damn sight easier with a narrow gauge than it is with a full track. Truth is, it only took three of us to get it jacked up. Getting the bent rail straight took more time." Stine dusted off his hands in an unconscious gesture, showing who had done most of the work.

"If Esther was kidnapped here, I ought to start looking here," Slocum said.

"Get your ass into the train, Slocum. We're going to camp. I want to keep my eye on you. I don't know you weren't in cahoots with those kidnapping sons of bitches," growled Atkinson. The railroad magnate climbed the steps and went into his personal car, slamming the door hard behind him.

"We can ride with the engineer in the cab," Stine said.

"I'm sorry this happened, Slocum. I know it's not your fault, but you have to see how Mr. Atkinson sees it."

"I rescued Mrs. Atkinson," Slocum said, marveling that Atkinson didn't seem to care one whit about his wife. If anything, he sounded kind of sour that Slocum had bothered returning her. "She's quite a woman—and she's mighty sick, too. She needs a doctor."

"She's fought off the ague for weeks," Stine said. "It won't kill her. She's a strong woman."

The locomotive hissed and shuddered and built up steam, then started backing down the tracks again. Slocum couldn't help staring out at the passing countryside, wondering where Esther had been taken. Whether Atkinson fired him or not, Slocum vowed to find the frisky little filly.

For his own peace of mind—and that of her mother. Somehow, pleasing Henrietta with the return of her daughter was more important than mending his own injured pride.

5

The Colorado and New Mexico railroad camp was like any of a dozen others Slocum had seen. The men were mostly Irish with a smattering of indeterminate mongrel thrown in with the remainder of the roughnecks. The stench of cabbage cooking was almost enough to turn his stomach. Slocum had boiled skunk cabbage more than once in the mountains to keep from starving. To actually eat cabbage was something akin to torture for him. None of the railroad men seemed to notice. If anything, they relished both smell and flavor from the way they wolfed down plates of corned beef and boiled cabbage.

"Yes, sirree," Abel Stine said enthusiastically to Slocum, "Mr. Atkinson feeds 'em good. The best chow any gandy dancers anywhere are likely to get."

"I'll take your word for it," Slocum said sarcastically. He was still madder than a wet hen over his treatment. He had rescued Henrietta Atkinson and hadn't gotten so much as a pat on the back over it. If anything, the dangerous rescue had been dismissed out of hand. All he had caught was hell from Atkinson for letting Carlos Villalobos kidnap Esther.

If she had been kidnapped. Slocum wondered what her

47

relationship was to Villalobos. She had never directly mentioned the man, saying only that she had been with Dunne. Slocum hesitated asking Stine, seeing how caught up he was in praising Clarence Atkinson. The foreman seemed to think the sun revolved around him.

"I need a horse so I can get back to where I might pick up the trail," Slocum said. He fumed at having to return to camp like this. It wasted precious time and made it all the more difficult to find Esther. The rocky ground had made tracking the two men who had kidnapped her mother difficult enough. He had gotten lucky and heard them bragging about how they were going to rape and kill her. By now, Esther's abductors could be all the way back to Pueblo or even halfway to Denver.

More than this, Slocum sensed undercurrents without having any real knowledge of what lay beneath seemingly peaceful waters.

"Go chow down, Slocum," Stine said. "I'll rustle you up a horse." The foreman set off, slapping men on the back and stopping to talk to others as he made his way across the camp. Slocum stared down a rocky draw to where blasting crews worked on the solid stone on this side of what had to be Cutthroat Gorge, putting in the final foundations for the bridge across to the far side. It was going to be a difficult project, but one that would look mighty pretty when finished. Slocum always enjoyed seeing a graceful arch of a bridge or the intricate crossing of timbers in a trestle.

He shivered thinking how close he had come to having one blown out from under him on the way here.

"Have some grub," a red-haired man said, shoving a tin plate of corned beef and cabbage at him. Slocum took it. His belly growled and overrode his distaste for the meal. A few bites and Slocum entirely forgot how he hated boiled cabbage.

"You been working for the C and NM long?" he asked his benefactor.

"About a year. I worked with Abel 'fore that. He's a decent man, maybe the best foreman I ever worked under. And I worked for some of the best. I was at Promontory Point when they drove the gold spike."

"Might be you can answer a question for me," Slocum said. He pointed toward Abel Stine. "Why's he wear that knit cap?"

"Well, now," the man said, sliding a little closer to Slocum and speaking in a conspiratorial whisper. "It's like this. It keeps his head warm!" The man laughed uproariously at his joke. Slocum didn't share in it. Seeing this, the man settled down and said, "If Abel gets to likin' you well enough, you might find out. Otherwise, not a man in this company'll tell you behind his back."

Slocum shrugged it off. Every railroad camp had its secrets, but this was downright odd. Stine wore that cap as if he had it nailed to the sides of his head.

"Thanks for the grub," he said, tossing the tin plate into a large pot with other plates for cleaning. "I've got to talk to Mr. Atkinson about some business." With that, he sauntered to the siding where the posh train had been backed in. Men swarmed over the engine, adjusting every possible nut and bolt. Two men used their chisel-like packing rods to be sure the hot boxes were stuffed with enough oil-soaked cotton to keep the wheels lubricated.

He went to the car used by Clarence Atkinson and climbed the narrow steps. Slocum started to knock, but the door was ajar. He intended to set matters right with the railroad owner before starting on the hunt for the man's daughter. Atkinson was obviously not in the car— but his wife was. She hunched over a writing desk at the side of the car, poring over an open ledger. She transferred numbers, scribbled furiously on a sheet of paper and then leaned back, frowning hard.

"Mrs. Atkinson?" Slocum called. "Excuse me. I wanted to see your husband."

"I don't know where he is," she said irritably. Then she heaved a sigh and leaned back. "I'm sorry to be so abrupt, Mr. Slocum. I haven't properly thanked you for saving me the way you did."

"Are you feeling better?" Slocum asked.

"The medicine works well," Henrietta said, smiling. The lovely brunette made a sweeping motion with her hand, dismissing his concerns. "Thank you for asking." In a voice almost too low for Slocum to hear, she added, "Clarence certainly never asked about my health."

"Are you working on the company books?" he asked.

Her eyebrows arched, and she moved her arms to cover the books. "I wasn't aware you were paying so much attention, sir."

"Why not?" Slocum smiled. How could any man ignore such a lovely woman?

"My father was a banker, and I assumed his job when he had a stroke. I learned a great deal about money and how to . . . use it," she said. "Of course, I was not allowed to actually run the bank. My brother did that, before he died suddenly."

"I'm sorry. So you do the railroad books?"

"If you are looking for my husband, try the mesa overlooking the camp. He often goes there to study the route." She folded the sheet of paper and tucked it into an envelope. "Is there anything else, Mr. Slocum?"

"No, I reckon not," Slocum said. He left her to her chores. Slocum began to get a different view of how much a genius Clarence Atkinson was. The man might be able to lay track, but it was apparent his wife took care of the money. With connections in the banking business, she might even raise capital for the C&NM to keep track being laid and bridges built—and repaired.

Slocum looked around. The sun dipped down behind

the mesa where Henrietta had said her husband often went. Not hearing his gruff voice in the camp, Slocum decided to hike up to the mesa. Even if Atkinson wasn't there, he could get a better idea of how the railroad was progressing. He might even see a way of getting back to the spot where Esther was kidnapped without having to ride back along the tracks. Any shortcut he could take now made rescuing the girl all the more likely.

Slocum found a game trail up the side of the hill. In the gathering darkness he had to pick his way carefully. He reached the top just as the sun vanished under this distant saw-toothed edge of the Rockies. His hand went to his Colt, but he didn't draw. Atkinson wasn't alone— but he didn't seem to be in any danger.

Not from the woman, whoever she was, unless her lips were painted with poison.

Slocum's climb to the mesa top had been quiet. He saw no reason to reveal himself. He moved like a shadow and got closer, spying on the railroad owner. Part of him rebelled at Atkinson for cheating on his wife like this, but another part told him eavesdropping might make piecing together the puzzle that was the Colorado and New Mexico railroad a whole lot easier.

No matter if he had suddenly turned into a feather-light Arapaho tracker, Slocum saw he couldn't get much closer to Atkinson and the woman still kissing him without revealing himself. He turned and wended his way back down the trail, mulling over what he had seen.

Atkinson was a damned fool for cheating on a woman as smart and pretty as Henrietta, but that wasn't what caused Slocum to wonder about the woman with the railroad owner. Where had the woman come from? She hadn't come on the train, and he doubted she was a resident of the camp. The men sat around their campfires swapping lies about woman. If she had been the camp whore, she wouldn't be with Clarence Atkinson.

"Hey, Slocum, got your nag for you. It took some doing but we found a saddle, too."

"Glad you did. I didn't cotton much to riding bareback through the mountains," he said.

"It's not much but until we can get supplies in from Denver, it'll have to do you." Stine handed the reins of a paint to Slocum. The horse turned a bored eye in his direction, then nickered softly. "When you heading out?"

"Soon as I can get some victuals for the saddlebags," Slocum said. "I might be on the trail for a spell and don't want to take time to hunt."

"That wouldn't be a good idea, hunting and all," Stine agreed. "The sound of a rifle might spook the varmints who stole away Miss Esther."

"You still think they work for Villalobos?"

"Who else?" Stine spat angrily, like a mad cat. He rubbed his fingers along the edges of his knit cap and pulled it down over his ears.

"You said Villalobos was trying to get across the gorge, but Atkinson beat him to this spot. Where's his camp?"

"Ten miles west of here, more or less," Stine said. "You don't think Villalobos would be dumb enough to take Miss Esther to his camp, do you?"

"It's a place to start," Slocum said, accepting a burlap bag loaded with food from an assistant cook. Slocum slung it over the back of the saddle, then mounted.

"Don't go getting lost or riding off the side of a cliff, Slocum," Stine said uneasily. "Might be best if you waited 'til dawn."

"Time's a'wasting," Slocum said, turning the paint's face and heading toward the base of the mesa. He had a few ideas where to begin his hunt and the trail left by the woman with Atkinson might be it.

As the sun rose, Slocum found the woman's tracks leading away from the back side of the mesa where she and At-

kinson had had their assignation the evening before. He
dismounted and studied them carefully, then shook his
head in wonder. A single rider—Slocum was sure it was
the woman—had ridden away to the north, heading along
the ridge that would eventually lead out of the mountains.
She was going somewhere else, but where? Pueblo? Denver? Or was she heading south once she got to the broad
stretch east of the Front Range?

"Or is she camped somewhere close by so she and Atkinson can meet whenever he wants?" Whatever the question, whatever the answer, it didn't seem to have anything
to do with Esther Atkinson's kidnapping. This was a solitary woman out alone, not someone who would have
taken the railroad magnate's daughter captive.

Slocum mounted and turned his paint's face toward the
west, following steep canyon trails and eventually arriving
at a point above Carlos Villalobos's camp just before sundown. Dropping to his belly to keep from silhouetting
himself against the sky and the full moon rising, Slocum
studied the tracks already down and the way the Mexican
railroader struggled to span Cutthroat Gorge. It didn't take
an engineer to see that Clarence Atkinson had reached a
far better location to cross the canyon. Villalobos had to
put up at least two extra supports on his trestle, causing
the span to be far more difficult and dangerous.

Counting the men in the camp, Slocum decided at least
ten of them were not working at laying track, preparing
foundations for the bridge or doing anything but lounging
about. To him that meant Villalobos was hiring gunmen.
Slocum snorted in disgust because he had already crossed
paths with several of them. Back in the Denver rail yard
and later when Stine had taken the gunfighters he had
retained to destroy some of Villalobos's rail.

"Killed the owlhoots outside Pueblo," Slocum mused.
"Would any of them remember me from Denver?"

It was a big gamble, but Slocum saw nothing standing

in the way of taking it. He was a risk taker by nature. Riding boldly into Villalobos's camp and asking for a job as a gunslinger might gain him entry and give him the chance to find Esther faster than skulking around. He stood, mounted, and put his plan—if it merited such a name—into effect.

He got within a hundred yards of the railroad camp when he saw men in the rocks leveling rifles at him. He stopped and waited until someone came out to see what he wanted.

"You got business here, mister?" asked a sturdy, well-built man ambling out from the camp. He wore a fancy bowler and an expensive coat. He might have looked out of place in the rough-and-tumble camp but he would have been right at home in a fancy Denver club. He certainly wasn't Carlos Villalobos.

"Who'm I talking to?" Slocum asked. "If you're looking to hire some guards, and you're the foreman, might be I do have business."

"That pretty much spells it out, now don't it?" the man said, pushing the bowler back on his forehead. He laughed. "You have a way of cutting right to the chase. I'm the foreman and Señor Villalobos *is* looking for some men capable with a side arm and rifle. You meet that requirement?"

Slocum cleared leather and had his six-shooter pointed square at the foreman's bowler before the man could blink. He raised his hand and shouted, "Whoa, fellas. Don't drill him. It's all right."

Slocum saw from the corner of his eye the guards lowering their rifles.

"You think you could have killed me and not been cut down?"

"Yep."

The foreman stared at him, then laughed. "You're a

cool one. Just the kind of *guard* we need. Climb out of the saddle."

Slocum dismounted and walked to the foreman.

"My name's Dunne. Who might you be?"

Slocum had thought that he faced was Dunne from all the fancy duds he wore, but was still taken aback. He covered his confusion quickly.

"I'm not too keen on giving out my name. Just call me John."

"All right, John. Have it your way. We don't much care if you give a summer name if you deliver the firepower when we ask you."

"What's the pay?"

"Fifty dollars a month," came the surprising reply. "That's a handsome sum, I know, but you'll earn it. Reckon you've heard we're fixing to go to war with the Atkinson boys."

"Heard tell of some dispute over territory. Don't know a danged thing about laying track," Slocum admitted.

"Just as well. Let Señor Villalobos worry about that, him or his nephew Paco."

"Paco?"

"Best damn engineer I ever worked with," Dunne said. "They worked on the Mexican Central 'fore coming to the U.S. and starting the Colorado Southern. If it wasn't for that fool Atkinson, we'd have track laid all the way in to the gold strike by now."

"None of that interests me. Do I take orders from you, Carlos, *and* Paco? That makes for a powerful lot of bosses."

"Paco stays to himself mostly. Planning the bridge is a full-time job. But if Señor Villalobos yells frog, you jump and don't come down 'til he tells you, is that clear?"

Slocum nodded. Others from the camp came out to see who Dunne had hired. He began worrying some of them might recognize him from the fight in the Denver rail yard, but he didn't recollect any of them and none of the gunmen raised the alarm about him.

"Go pitch your gear yonder, John," said Dunne. "You want to do some target practice, get a rifle and ammo from the quartermaster. Or you can just set up a target on your own down in that wash."

"Why there?" asked Slocum.

"It's away from the camp, and there's not much chance of a ricochet hitting any of the men working to lay track."

"Anywhere off limits?"

"Stay out of the way of men who are actually putting in a day's work," spoke up a burly man who had the look of a railroader about him. Huge hands callused from lugging steel rail tightened into fists. The cracking of bones alerted Slocum to the man's strength.

"This here's Matthews, my assistant," Dunne said. "He does the real work around here—to hear him tell it."

Matthews growled deep in his throat. Slocum wondered if he ought to simply shoot the man now as insurance against him finding some reason to lock those meaty fingers around Slocum's own throat. The assistant foreman spun and stalked off, his big feet crunching gravel as he went.

"Angry man," Slocum observed.

"He doesn't like the way we're hiring men like you. Matthews likes a fight now and then, but only when he's drunk and in a saloon. It sticks in his craw what Atkinson has done and that we have to defend ourselves."

"Understandable," Slocum said. As they walked into the camp, he looked around for anywhere Esther might be imprisoned. The only possible place was in Villalobos's personal railroad car on a siding. From the quick look he got at it, this parlor car might have been built by the same company that had put together Clarence Atkinson's.

Slocum hoped it had been. That would make it easier for him to search later on.

"Pitch your gear anywhere you want. The corral for your horse is back down the tracks a couple hundred yards. We keep the animals there so they won't be too spooked when we blast."

"Real thoughty of you," Slocum said.

"You got a mouth on you," Dunne said. "Don't let it get in the way of doing your job."

Slocum spread his bedroll, ground cloth first, and then his blanket. The rocky ground was uncomfortable, but he wasn't inclined to go to sleep. Not yet. He lay staring at the stars and listening to the sounds of the camp. The railroad workers drifted to sleep first, tuckered out from a day of hard, backbreaking work. One by one, the hired gunmen also went to sleep, snoring loud enough to drown out the mournful yowls of distant coyotes. A wind picked up and whistled through Cutthroat Gorge a quarter mile off, sounding like a consumptive man trying to breathe, but Slocum wasn't straining to hear wind or animal.

He listened for any sound, however small, that would tell him where Esther Atkinson might be. And it didn't come. He rolled onto his side so he could look at the fancy car on the siding. That was the only place where she might be held prisoner. The smaller shacks laden with dynamite and supplies had been opened and closed dozens of times since he'd arrived. Even if everyone in the camp knew they held a prisoner, one of the men would have made some comment.

Especially about a woman as pretty as Esther Atkinson.

It was past midnight when Slocum slipped out from under his blanket and carefully walked to the railroad car. He pressed his hand against the side to guide him in the darkness. The moon that had been so bright earlier now vanished behind clouds promising a mountain storm. If he rescued Esther, they could escape under the cover of a downpour. But first he had to find her.

Slocum walked to the rear of the parlor car, then mounted the steps to the rear platform. Testing the doorknob showed it was unlocked. He peered through the glass in the door, but the unlit interior refused to give up any secrets. He took a deep breath, turned the knob, and pushed the door inward.

As he did, he heard the telltale sound of a six-shooter cocking.

"What the hell do you think you're doing?" came Dunne's cold voice from behind Slocum.

6

Slocum froze. He could never throw down on Dunne, not when the man already had the drop on him.

"What are you doing? Breaking into Señor Villalobos's car?" demanded Dunne.

"I'm not breaking in," Slocum lied, his mind racing to find a plausible reason for sneaking into the private car. "The door was open, and I got suspicious."

"He doesn't lock it. You were going in to steal whatever wasn't nailed down." Hardness came to the well-dressed foreman's voice now, and Slocum knew he had to think up another lie fast.

"No, no," Slocum denied, hoping he sounded sincere. "I heard someone moving around inside. I was afraid there was a sneak thief loose in the camp."

"The only thief I see is you," Dunne said.

"There!" Slocum said, holding the door half open. "Did you hear it? Someone's still inside." There hadn't been any sound in the car, but Slocum banked on the natural sounds all around to mask that. The wind gusting through the distant canyon provided an almost constant moaning sound like a man in pain. Other sounds came from the dying campfires and the men tossing and turning on the hard ground as they slept. It all mixed together in what Slocum hoped was enough of a confusion of noise to distract Dunne.

"I did hear something," Dunne said unexpectedly. "Get back. I'll go in and check it out."

The foreman pushed past Slocum, giving him a look that might have melted a steel railroad spike, then kicked open the door and called, "Who's in there?"

Something crashed loudy inside, startling both Dunne and Slocum. Slocum had not thought anyone was inside—anyone but perhaps Esther Atkinson. She might be trying to free herself from bonds.

"Freeze, John. I'll take care of this. The boss doesn't like just anybody nosing around," Dunne said, stopping Slocum from pulling out his six-shooter. All Slocum could do was hang back and listen. If Esther was prisoner inside, Dunne would know it. The foreman's actions struck Slocum as odd, though. He'd know it was the girl trying to escape, but his expression of surprise had been real. Slocum had sat across from enough men playing poker to know when a man was faking a reaction and when one was real. Well, with maybe one exception.

Dunne thought something was wrong inside. If Esther had been there, he would have chased Slocum off. Instead, the foreman called out to Slocum.

"John, circle around and cut off any varmint tryin' to escape!"

Slocum vaulted the low iron railing at the rear of the car and landed hard on the rocky ground. He got his feet under him, drew his six-gun, and ran to the front of the car. Ready to stop anyone from leaving, he leveled his six-shooter at the door and waited.

"Don't shoot," came Dunne's order after almost a minute. "It's me. I'm coming out." The door swung open, and the foreman poked his head out fast, darting back like a striking snake. When he saw that Slocum recognized him and wasn't going to shoot, he exited the car.

"Damnedest thing I ever saw. I think someone was inside, but where'd he go? This isn't a haunted camp, and no ghost'd be in the boss's car. Nobody's ever been killed there."

The only thing Slocum could think was opening the rear door had let in a gust of wind that had knocked over something inside the luxury car. Dunne had believed the story of a prowler inside and had gone in to investigate, letting Slocum off the hook.

"Might be hiding inside. If he didn't go past you and out the back way or come out the front, that's the only explanation," Slocum said, wanting an excuse to look in the car. Dunne might be trying to hide Esther's presence inside.

That idea came crashing down to earth when the foreman gestured with his pistol for Slocum to follow. Together they searched every nook and cranny of the railroad car. As far as Slocum could tell, Esther had never been kept there as a prisoner.

"I don't get it. You heard someone in here and so did I. Somebody knocked over that vase. Señor Villalobos is going to be mad as hell over it getting broke," Dunne said, looking at the pieces on the floor. "What are we going to tell him? That we let some yahoo waltz in here and then get away without us even laying eyes on him?"

"Tell him the wind blew open the door and knocked over the vase," Slocum said. He thought that was the literal truth, but he said it in such a way that it sounded like a lie to Dunne.

"What else can we do?" the foreman asked. He pushed the bowler back on his head and wiped sweat off his forehead, in spite of the chilly night. Slocum saw the man was frightened of Villalobos and what he might say about any slip in security around the camp. "Get back to sleep. If you hear any more noises, let me know right away.

Don't go chasing off after it on your own. That's a good way to catch a bullet in the back."

"All right," Slocum agreed. He gave the car one last quick once-over and assured himself that Esther Atkinson hadn't been here. But if Esther Atkinson wasn't here, where was she?

"Where's Villalobos?" he asked suddenly. "And his nephew?"

"They're on the other side of Cutthroat Gorge," Dunne said. "They have to do some surveying and testing of the rock. I don't know what he does, but Señor Villalobos is a real *brujo* when it comes to figuring out how strong rock is."

"How long does it take to get to the other side of the canyon?" Slocum asked.

"Almost two days. The pair of 'em went down this side on ropes, then scaled the far side. Don't ask me how."

"You saw them?"

"I watched every inch of the climb up. Took 'em hours and hours. They went up like spiders against the rock."

Slocum frowned. If Villalobos and his nephew had been gone for two days to survey the far side of the canyon, that removed them from being present at Esther's kidnapping. But then, Villalobos need only give the orders. He had no reason to take part in the crime personally.

"I'm turning in," Slocum said, suddenly very tired. He couldn't make head nor tail out of any of this.

"Yeah, go on. I'll see that extra guards are posted."

Slocum stayed awake long enough to see that Dunne did as he said. And none of the guards were sent to protect the secrecy of Esther Atkinson's captivity that Slocum could see.

The girl simply was not being held in Villalobos's camp. With that thought rattling around in his head, Slocum drifted into an uneasy, nightmare riddled sleep.

* * *

Slocum awoke just before dawn to the sound of the cook preparing breakfast. All Slocum could say about it was that he didn't have to face another plate of corned beef and cabbage. What the mess was, he couldn't say, but it went down all right and didn't kick around in his belly once there. Most of the men finished their chuck and went to work, leveling the railroad bed, moving steel rails, swinging heavy hammers into spikes to hold the steel to the wooden railroad ties.

Slocum and the others entrusted with guarding the camp assembled in the wash Dunne had mentioned the day before. The foreman looked dapper in his fancy duds, but Slocum saw the dark circles under his eyes that betrayed a sleepless night.

"Gents, you got a hard job ahead of you. We been having theft and curious goings-on in the camp." Dunne glanced in Slocum's direction, as if telling him not to comment more on what had happened in Villalobos's car the night before. That was the last thing in the world Slocum would do. He didn't want it getting out he was prowling around, snooping where he shouldn't.

"We got paid good money, Dunne," said a tough-looking man with two six-shooters shoved into his belt. "I hanker for some action, not settin' round this worthless camp. Who do we shoot and when?"

"We got a war brewing with a rival gang," Dunne said grimly. "We aren't looking for trouble. Clarence Atkinson and his men are."

Slocum fought to keep from laughing out loud. Dunne made it sound as if Atkinson was the source of the trouble when it was the other way around. Villalobos was responsible for stirring up the bad blood. Kidnapping Henrietta Atkinson was only part of it. He still held Esther Atkinson captive.

Somewhere.

Slocum vowed to find out where and return her to her parents.

"I want patrols out. Get up high in the rock with rifles so you can see every approach to camp. We got a shipment of rail and wood coming in later today. If anything happens to it, we will be set back a week or more getting across Cutthroat Gorge," Dunne said. "Get out there and keep an eagle eye for trouble. All of you."

Slocum took a rifle from the opened case at Dunne's feet. He loaded it and looked around for a likely spot to stand sentry duty. More than this, he wanted a place where he could spy on the camp. Esther might not be in the camp but some of Villalobos's men might be holding her nearby.

All day Slocum prowled like a hunting cougar—to no avail. He was footsore from tramping around in the rocks, and his eyes burned from squinting into the sun. He was beginning to doubt Villalobos had anything to do with Esther's kidnapping.

"Time for grub," called the cook.

Slocum heard a whisper pass through the men lining up to get their vittles. He turned to see a small, dirty man strutting into camp from the direction of the gorge. His clothing was torn and his hands cut in places, but the smile on his face was shining bright. He was a handsome enough man with black hair in wild disarray.

"Gentlemen, I have good news!" the man cried. "My uncle has found the perfect spot to cross this hole in the ground. We will build and do it easily and quickly with a new design. Dunne, Matthews, where are you, amigos?"

The foreman and his assistant rushed out.

"You're back early," Dunne said. "Your uncle led us to believe you'd be a few more days, Paco."

"Pah, why take so much time when we can cross in days! We will build the bridge to my uncle, and he will ride back across in his very own locomotive!"

A cheer went up. Slocum nudged the man next to him in line.

"That's Paco Villalobos?"

"None other than. He's a pistol, that boy. Don't look like much, but I never seen a better railroad engineer. Not the kind in the cab, the kind what builds the road. He can eyeball the land and know exactly the right place to build fast and secure. It's a gift, I tell you. I seen men twenty years in the business that can't match him."

Before Slocum could reply, a thunderous explosion rocked the camp. He turned and caught a cloud of dust and flying rock splinters in the face. He staggered back, gasping for air. The confusion that spread through the camp told him this wasn't anything planned.

"There wasn't no blastin' bein' done!"

"The magazine blew," shouted Dunne. "Get over there and see if anything can be salvaged."

Slocum followed the horde of workers who had dropped their tin plates and rushed to the powder magazine. A spark could set off a magazine, or a lucifer carelessly tossed by a guard. When Slocum got to the top of the rise looking down into the hollow where Villalobos had put his explosives, Slocum saw there'd be no way to ever tell what had happened. A twenty foot crater remained. Nothing more. Every stick of dynamite, every keg of blasting powder, all had blown, sending out the curtain of dust and rock that had engulfed the camp.

"This is a disaster," cried Paco Villalobos. "We need to blast to put in the foundations for my bridge. No, this will not do. I will not permit this thing to happen!" He launched into Spanish. Slocum understood one word in ten but didn't have to be fluent in the language to know Paco Villalobos was cursing everyone and everything for this misfortune.

"We'll get more powder from Pueblo right away,"

Dunne said. "It'll put us behind schedule only a couple days. Honest, Señor, only a couple days."

"Who would do this thing?" Paco spun around and, like a compass needle came to face in the direction of the Colorado and New Mexico camp. "He did it. That devil Atkinson is responsible!"

Slocum wondered if Abel Stine might have sent men out to blow the magazine. It certainly crippled Villalobos's ability to cross the gorge, but Stine knew Slocum was out hunting for Esther. Would he do anything to jeopardize her rescue?

Walking around the perimeter of the blast, Slocum found the evidence that this had been sabotage. A trail of black powder had been laid from high in the rocks to the shed. The remains of a lucifer showed where the crude fuse had been ignited.

"What'd you find, John?" asked Dunne. Slocum silently pointed.

"Son of a bitch! Paco was right. Atkinson did this!"

Slocum wasn't going to argue the point. Someone had blown up the powder magazine, and it might have been men sent out by Atkinson. Though he didn't think so unless something more was in the wind.

"Camp," Slocum said. "Get back to camp. This is a diversion!"

He drew his Colt Navy as he ran. The sound of sledgehammers swinging against steel reached his ears before he saw the men systematically destroying the engine, knocking off pressure vales and bending drive rods and pistons. Without thinking, Slocum squeezed off a shot that *pinged!* off the side of the engine. These might be Stine's men, but Slocum was offended by the way they were skulking around. He had helped destroy a shipment of rails to Villalobos's camp, and had not cottoned much to it.

Better to face your opponent and have it out than to sneak around behind his back.

The single shot caused the men to turn and run. Slocum fired a couple more times at them but they hightailed it back down the tracks.

"Cowards," growled Paco Villalobos. "Stay and fight!" he shouted after them. The fiery Mexican grabbed a rifle from Dunne and fired after them. He lowered it and said, "They will not escape. We will not permit it. Get the handcar on the tracks. We will chase them and kill them for what they have done."

"That's not smart," Slocum started. Paco ignored him. He had vengeance on his mind and nothing else. The workers got two handcars onto the tracks. Paco jumped onto the first with a half dozen guards. Dunne motioned to Slocum to join him on the second.

By the time the men got to pumping hard and sent the handcar sailing down the tracks, the one Paco rode was already out of sight.

"Speed it up, Dunne," Slocum said. "This doesn't feel right to me."

"Hell, why should it? They blew up our powder and hammered away at our locomotive. They've sabotaged our equipment and—" Dunne's tirade was cut off by gunfire ahead.

The foreman looked up, startled. The wind caught his bowler and sent it sailing back down the track. He grabbed instinctively for it, and that saved his life. As he bent, a bullet ripped through the air where his face had been a fraction of a second earlier.

"Get off the car," Slocum shouted, abandoning the handcar in favor of taking cover alongside the tracks. So much lead flew through the air he thought he was caught in some unholy, unnatural hailstorm.

"They set up an ambush," Slocum told Dunne when the foreman scrambled over behind a rock a few feet away.

"They lured us from camp. They intended to plug who-ever followed them."

"Sons of bitches," grumbled Dunne. "And I lost my gun."

Slocum tossed the man his rifle and drew his six-shooter. He had fired it several times but didn't have time to reload, not if he wanted to get into position fast.

"I'm circling. Hold them down," Slocum said. He didn't wait to see if Dunne went along with the plan. He darted out from cover, dancing around as a fusillade of slugs sought his flesh. He stumbled when one hit his boot heel, then he was safe behind a large boulder. Slocum wasted no time thanking his lucky stars for quick feet and poor marksmanship on the part of his attackers. He climbed the sheer face of the rock using strong fingers and the toes of his boots in almost imperceptible hollows. He tumbled onto the top of the rock and found himself in perfect range for the three men crouched nearby.

Slocum got his six-gun out again and fired twice. One bushwhacker looked down at his chest, startled at the sud-den blossoming of red from his chest. He touched the spot in disbelief, then sank to the ground, dead without know-ing it.

The other two with him turned their rifles on Slocum. And Slocum's six-shooter came up empty, forcing him to retreat back down the rock. Cursing, he took the time to reload. By the time he got back to his position on top of the boulder, the men were gone. They had even taken the body of their confederate with them.

Slocum's frustration knew no bounds. He had the right idea but had rushed into the fight with only two rounds in his pistol. If he had taken time or had even brought the rifle with him, three of the men would be pushing up daisies now.

He listened and heard only sporadic gunfire, all coming from the direction of Villalobos's men.

"Dunne!" he shouted. "They've hightailed it. Stop shooting. Get your men to stop firing."

Dunne barked out the command. Only when there hadn't been a shot fired in almost a minute did Slocum show himself.

"They went up into the high ground," Slocum said. "Give me a half dozen men, and I can track them."

"In this country? Don't be dumb, John. You don't know the land, do you?"

"No, but—"

"Forget it. They might want us to split our forces and attack again. Stick around the camp. We need to protect what they haven't blown up or pounded into rivets," said Dunne.

There was something in what the foreman said, as much as Slocum wanted to track down the bushwhackers. He wanted to know if Stine had sent them and risked Esther's life.

Or if these owlhoots played a different game entirely.

Slocum helped push the handcar they had ridden off the tracks while Dunne moved down the tracks. So much lead had ripped through it, the wood platform had been blown away. Trying to ride it back would have taken longer than walking.

"No!" came Dunne's anguished cry. "It can't be. No, no, no!"

Slocum rushed down the tracks, six-shooter out. He slid it back into his cross-draw holster when he saw there wasn't any danger. Not now. Dunne stood over the body of Paco Villalobos. The Mexican had been filled with so much lead that Slocum wouldn't have recognized him as human if he hadn't known who he was.

"They killed him. They murdered him," Dunne said. "As God is my witness, I won't let them get by with this. They'll pay. By damn, I'll make Atkinson pay with his life for this!"

7

"What's Carlos going to say? I can't tell him," moaned Dunne. "Paco was his favorite nephew, the only one in his entire family who had gone into railroad construction. And the kid was a genius. Never saw anyone that good. But he's dead." Dunne put his head in his hands. Slocum had seldom seen anyone so affected by a man's death. It was hard to believe this man had tried to kill him at least once and was probably responsible for the bomb that blew up the bridge with Atkinson's train—and men—on it.

He remembered back to Little Ben's death and knew he carried the seeds of that pain within him and would for some time. Maybe it had been the same with Dunne and Villalobos's nephew.

"Let me see if I can't track them down," Slocum said. "I'm good. Even if they turned to ghosts and floated across solid rock, I can track them."

Dunne looked up. "I'm offering a thousand dollar reward, John. Bring them back, dead or alive don't make no never mind to me, and the reward's yours. Take any of the men you want with you."

"I travel better alone," Slocum said. "Too many with me and I become a target."

"It's better for them to guard the camp. We don't want any more sabotage. I should have had guards posted at the powder magazine. I should never have let Paco run off like that. He was a hothead. Carlos is going to blame me."

"It wasn't your fault. Nobody in the camp will say it was," Slocum said. How like the same speech he had given to Abel Stine!

"He's right, Dunne," piped up Matthews. "We all wanted blood after they blowed up our powder. I wanted to rip 'em apart with my own hands. Never thought we'd be goin' into a trap. Paco never did, I never did. How could you?"

"John tried to warn me."

"I'm a cautious man by nature," Slocum lied. He was anything but cautious, but he was never foolhardy when his life rode on his quick decisions. "Can I get after them?"

"Go on, take what supplies you'll need. But bring them back. I don't want them turned over to any lawman. I want their heads thrown into the canyon and don't much care if their bodies are still attached when they hit bottom."

Slocum mounted his paint, leaving a camp for the second time in three days. Curiously, leaving felt the same both times. He rode out to avenge a wrong. He had not found Esther, but he hadn't found evidence anyone in Villalobos's camp had been responsible for her kidnapping. Now he sought the trail left by Paco Villalobos's killers. He wondered if it led back to Atkinson's camp.

Three hours later, he gave up on tracking the killers. They had ridden fast and hard, possibly having spare horses with them to give them the edge in escaping. The attack on Villalobos's camp had been well planned and executed. Whether they had intended to kill Paco Villalobos was something Slocum couldn't tell. The railroad builder's nephew had only just returned to camp, so the bushwhackers couldn't be sure he'd be there. His murder was icing on a cake that Slocum wanted to stuff down the killers' throats. If he could figure out who they were.

He turned his horse back toward Atkinson's camp. There were questions to ask and answers to be considered before he condemned the man for the ambush.

Nothing about the war between the two railroad companies made much sense. Kidnapping without any trace, murder, and sabotage neither seemed to do. He vowed to get to the bottom of it, if not for Esther's sake, then to satisfy his own curiosity and sense of justice.

It was past noon when Slocum rode into the C&NM camp. He looked around for any sign of the men he had futilely tracked. Had they come back here or were they still in the mountains? Slocum identified all the men Stine had hired as guards who had been in the camp when he had left earlier. No new faces—but maybe they were the ones responsible for killing Paco.

"Slocum, what luck? You find Miss Esther?" came Stine's anxious question.

"Tried but no luck yet," Slocum said, dismounting. "You send out any men to find her?"

Stine shook his head. "I'm keeping close to camp to hold down sabotage. Somebody set fire to a pile of ties we had allotted for the bridge repair. If one of the guards hadn't spotted it, we'd've had to wait for hell to freeze over 'fore getting new ones. Would have had to rebuild the bridge from the other side."

"You send any men into Villalobos's camp?"

"Why? Is Esther there?"

"Not so fast. I got into the camp but didn't find any trace of her. If Villalobos had anything to do with kidnapping her, he's holding her somewhere else."

"Of course he took her! Who else could it be?"

To that Slocum had no answer.

"I'm not giving up, but I don't think Villalobos is responsible." Slocum stared squarely at Stine and asked again, "You sure you didn't send anyone over to his camp to do some mischief?"

"None of my boys," Stine said. He tugged at his knit cap, pulling it down a little more over his ears. "I need all the hands I can get to repair the bridge. Without it back in place, we're stranded here. We need supplies bad, and they have to come in from Pueblo or Denver. If we don't bring 'em in by rail, we'd have to do all our supplying over mountain passes on mule back."

"Who, other than Villalobos, wants to stop you from getting across Cutthroat Gorge?" asked Slocum.

Stine rubbed his stubbled chin as he thought. "Don't know there's anyone else. Now don't you get started on blaming Jay Gould for everything. He's one mean hombre, but he's occupied with digesting the Union Pacific shares he bought. And General Palmer plays, but not crooked. Never heard a thing nasty about the way he takes over another railroad."

Slocum put the paint into the corral and spent the next couple hours going around the camp, listening to what the workers had to say and what they didn't.

Most of their gossip was about Esther Atkinson. Missing was any hint of bragging over a successful raid on Villalobos's camp. If any of the men had heard even a whisper about such an expedition against their hated rival, they would be talking about it. Some of the men put forth the notion they ought to lay down their picks and shovels and march over to give Villalobos what for, but Slocum knew this was only hot air.

No one knew anything about the attack that had killed Paco Villalobos, just as no one in the rival camp seemed to know anything about Esther's kidnapping.

Slocum went to find Clarence Atkinson and clear the

air. He had to know if the railroad magnate had hired men from outside to make the raid.

Rapping on the door to Atkinson's car, he waited until the man growled for him to enter.

"You," Clarence Atkinson said, glaring at him. "You have any news about my daughter, or did you come to ask for more money?"

"I was on the trail but lost it," Slocum said, seeing no reason to deny it. "I trailed her from the camp, but this is mighty rocky soil around here." Slocum started to say something about the woman he had seen Atkinson with, but decided to keep that as a hole card.

"What do you want, if it's not to tell me my daughter is safe?"

Slocum studied the man for a moment. Atkinson was bluff and gruff but wasn't entirely in control of his own railroad. Slocum had seen that Henrietta Atkinson had a great deal to do with the finances. Without Abel Stine there might not have been such progress laying track. And how had Atkinson gotten to this spot ahead of Villalobos? This was the safest, easiest way across Cutthroat Gorge, if any bridge building project in these mountains could be called safe.

That was the evidence, but Slocum saw none of it as flowing directly from Atkinson's hand. Unlike Villalobos, Atkinson let others do his work.

"Did you send men to Villalobos's camp yesterday?" Slocum asked.

"What? Why, no. Everyone's been here, I think." He sputtered a moment and then regained his composure. "What is it you want to know, Slocum?"

"You didn't send anyone out to blow up Villalobos's powder magazine?"

"No, but it is a good idea, unless . . ."

"Unless what?"

"He might have Esther there. I wouldn't put it past that

bastard! I should send my men over and—"

"Don't bother," Slocum said. "Esther's not there. I scouted the entire camp."

"What do you want, Slocum? Tell me. I am a busy man."

"Think I found out," Slocum said, leaving without Atkinson telling him to go. Outside in the warm Colorado sun, he looked around and saw how everyone went about their jobs. They struggled on two fronts, one ahead and the other behind. There weren't that many extra men to launch the attack against Villalobos. While Atkinson might have hired others from Pueblo or some other town in central Colorado to attack his rival's camp, Slocum doubted it.

Atkinson would have brought the men here. And how would he have contacted them if the idea of an attack had come to him after the bridge had been blown up and his daughter taken captive? It was a ways overland.

"The woman might be a courier," he mused. That was the only way Atkinson could have sent out word to attack Villalobos.

If he had.

Slocum was dog tired and found a spot in the shade to curl up, but sleep didn't come easily. His mind turned over every possible facet of this curious problem. Villalobos hadn't kidnapped Esther. Who had? Atkinson hadn't murdered Paco. Who had?

There had been mutual attacks. Slocum had taken part in one outside Pueblo, and he knew Dunne had led the assault on him and Stine in the Denver rail yard. This sparked another memory, of Esther with Dunne. Should he have mentioned her kidnapping to Dunne to see what the foreman's reaction would have been?

The answers danced just beyond Slocum's grasp as he drifted to sleep, only to awaken near dusk. He yawned, stretched and got up, not sure what he ought to do next.

He had come to the end of the trail hunting for Esther unless something new turned up. For the life of him, Slocum couldn't figure what that might be.

He headed for the grub being dished out by the cook. At least tonight's fare wasn't the damnable corned beef and cabbage, though Slocum was hungry enough to eat his own boots. As he headed for the chow line, someone called his name. He turned and saw Henrietta Atkinson standing on the rear platform of the last car.

"Mr. Slocum, may I have a word with you?" She motioned him over.

"Evening, ma'am," he said, politely touching the brim of his dusty Stetson as he stood at the bottom of the steps.

"Come in, please," she said. "I want to talk to you."

He followed her into the car. She shut the door. He inhaled and sniffed the violet-scented perfume she used. It was heady for a man who had spent the last three days riding back and forth and smelling nothing but the coppery tang of spilled blood and acrid gunpowder.

More than this, she was a handsome woman who was obviously worried about her daughter.

"I haven't found anything," Slocum said, cutting to the chase. He saw no reason to waltz around with pleasantries. The sooner he got back in the saddle, now that he was rested, the sooner he would find Esther.

"You are a blunt man," Henrietta said, smiling slightly. "Clarence is like that, but without your charm."

"Charm?" Slocum had to laugh. "Can't rightly say anyone's accused me of having charm before."

"Come now, sir. That delightful Southern accent, your manners, both set you apart from the roughnecks working on a railroad. And you are accomplished with your side arm. I can tell by its worn handle."

Slocum had nothing to say.

"Sit down and tell me what you've found out. Even if

you think it's nothing, perhaps a tiny clue will mean something to me."

He sat on the edge of her bed, wondering if he ought to mention seeing her husband with the woman on the mesa.

"You *have* uncovered something, haven't you? I can tell that you don't want to worry me."

"I haven't found anything positive," Slocum admitted. She sat beside him on the bed, her leg pressing into his warmly. "All I seem to have done is show what *isn't*. That's not very much."

"What 'isn't'?" she asked in a soft voice. She laid her hand on his arm, then moved it to his leg. Slocum began to get uncomfortable. Henrietta Atkinson was as attractive as her daughter and, truth to tell, he found her more appealing than Esther. They looked alike but there the similarity ended. Henrietta was caring and alive. Slocum got the feeling Esther was a scheming termagant who always got her way. And if she didn't, there would be hell to pay.

But Henrietta? She was genuinely worried over her daughter's disappearance. Slocum wondered if she knew her husband was cheating on her with another woman, the one he had seen with Clarence Atkinson on the mesa. He didn't feel as if he were retribution. She made him feel he was the only man in the world.

"Well," Slocum said, shifting his weight to try to move away from Henrietta. "It's like this. I got into Villalobos's camp, and there was no trace of your daughter. I don't think he had anything to do with taking her."

"If Villalobos did not do it, then who did?" She half closed her eyes and pursed her lips; her kissable, ruby lips.

"I don't know," Slocum said, feeling himself melting inside as her charm radiated outward. "I don't know much other than I want to do this." He put his arm around her and pulled Henrietta close. Their lips touched. The spark of desire turned into a raging forest fire.

She returned the kiss with as much passion as Slocum delivered it. Maybe more. She pressed hard against him, and he felt her firm, full breasts crushing into his chest. They sank back to the bed, lying side by side as their hands began exploring each other's body. Slocum had a pang of guilt about what they did. Henrietta was a married woman.

Atkinson might be cheating on her, but it wasn't right that he cuckold him. Somehow, this thought vanished as Henrietta found all the right places to touch and stroke and caress. Her cheek brushed his beard-stubbled one before her tongue lightly slipped in and out of his ear.

"Like that, John. I want you to take me like that, only here," she said, pulling his hand up under her skirts. "And with this." She shifted position so she could work her hand into his unbuttoned fly and grasp his manhood. "Gently, slowly, don't hurry. I want to experience it all."

"I can't do this," Slocum started.

"You must!" she cried. "I'm going crazy with need. Clarence avoids me like the plague."

Slocum couldn't figure out why the railroad magnate would deny such a lovely woman as the one Slocum now held in his arms and whose privates pressed against his so intimately. She was passionate and lovely and intelligent and . . . he lost all his reservations when she repositioned herself just enough to allow his hardness to slip inside her most intimate recess.

They gasped in unison at the intrusion. Then Slocum's body took over from his mind. He reached around her and pushed her skirts out of the way. His hands found the naked flesh of her rump. Pulling her strongly toward him caused an even deeper penetration that thrilled them both. Slocum kissed and licked at the woman's swanlike throat and her lips and eyes before rolling atop her.

Henrietta's legs parted even wider in wanton invitation. No man could refuse, and Slocum wasn't going to try. As her knees came up on either side of his body, he levered his hips forward and began grinding about, like a spoon in a mixing bowl.

"Oh, yes, John. I need this. I *need* it! Don't you dare stop."

Slocum was past the point of volition. He began rocking to and fro, his hips taking on a life of their own. Heat built in his loins as he moved faster. Henrietta tried to slow him down—and he tried so he could prolong the exquisite sensations mounting within him.

"Yes, oh, yes, now!" she gasped out, giving him the signal to go all out. She became a bucking bronco under him. Slocum held on and rode hard until there was nothing left but the memory of intense pleasure in both of them.

Henrietta gasped and moaned and finally subsided. Slocum dropped to the bed beside her, arms cradling her.

"I feel so safe and secure with you. I used to feel that way with Clarence," she said in a tiny voice. Henrietta didn't have to add that this was no longer what she felt toward her husband. It still bothered Slocum that she was married, but not as much as it had.

"I'll find your daughter," he promised, not sure how he was going to deliver on this vow since he had exhausted all the possibilities. Whoever had kidnapped her had not made any ransom demand.

That set Slocum to thinking that Esther Atkinson might not have been kidnapped at all.

And then he wasn't thinking about much of anything but the woman crushed against him and her insistent new demands on him.

8

Slocum stayed in the C&NM camp until the next morning, having sneaked from Henrietta Atkinson's parlor car sometime after two in the morning. He felt damned guilty about what they had done, her being a married woman, but the glow within and the feeling he had somehow soothed her when her husband could not helped lessen the wrongdoing.

What would not go away was the sense of failure he felt returning Esther to her parents. He had run dry of ideas of where to look for her.

One notion kept rearing its ugly head, though. If Villalobos had nothing to do with taking the young woman, perhaps she had run off on her on. She had shown herself to be strong willed and obstinate, used to getting her own way. "A spoiled little rich girl," Slocum muttered to himself. That was Esther Atkinson.

He considered getting on the paint horse and just riding, heading west, getting into Ute country and pushing across the Nevada desert until he reached California. He had not been to the Pacific Coast in years. It wasn't right fooling around with another man's wife, especially one as rich and powerful as Clarence Atkinson, and if the man's daughter had lit out on her own, Slocum's chance of finding her was slim.

If he kept poking around, he'd find himself the target of both railroad camps. Villalobos would come after him as one of Atkinson's hired guns, and Atkinson would want blood because Slocum had not returned his daughter.

Slocum's mind wandered down other corridors. Could Esther's disappearance and Paco Villalobos's murder be tied together? If some third party, like Jay Gould, wanted the two companies at each other's throats, this was the way to do it. Destroy equipment, threaten families, get both sides riled up to the point of shooting anything that moved. Slocum couldn't see exactly how even Gould would profit. Better to let the two railroad companies race across Cutthroat Gorge, then buy out the winner. That saved the trouble of having to design and build the trestle and allowed the powerful narrow gauge engines to huff and puff directly to the gold strikes for their loads of ore.

He waved to Abel Stine, then turned his paint back along the tracks. He wasn't certain what he intended to do. Ride a spell, then decide. By midday he ought to have made up his mind. The one thorn in his notion of simply riding away and leaving it all behind was the chance that Esther Atkinson *had* been kidnapped and needed his help.

Henrietta had asked most persuasively for his aid. If Esther needed rescuing, he ought to do it. Of all the men in Atkinson's camp, he was the best suited for the chore. The rest were mostly all railroad men, the so-called guards from Denver having been killed when the locomotive tumbled into the canyon after the bridge was blown out from under them. Stine had no more than three others in camp to stand guard for him.

"Can't do it," he said in disgust. "There's no way I can let them down. Any of them," he said, including not only the Atkinsons but Abel Stine, as well.

Slocum forced himself to stop turning over the problem

in his mind. He simply rode, eyeing the terrain for rattlers
and holes his horse might step into. He rocked gently with
the horse's gait and drifted along. It wasn't much of a
surprise to him when he discovered he was working his
way out of the mountains and back into the flats where
he could turn south to head into New Mexico through
Raton Pass or north to Pueblo.

"If there's a clue about Esther's whereabouts, it'll be
north," he decided.

It took five more days to reach the thriving steel town.
Slocum saw the pillars of ugly black smoke curling up
from the foundries and ore mills long before he spotted
the town. Pueblo lay in a shallow depression, trapping
even more of the filthy smoke gushing from its industry.

But with that soot and smoke came wealth, vast wealth.
Every ounce of ore from the California Gulch came first
to Pueblo before being shipped to the banks in Denver.
Silver from other mines rattled by narrow gauge from the
mountains and into the smelters. Most of all, as far as the
railroaders were concerned, the factories producing steel
rail were the real gold mines that let them continue their
relentless push into every nook and cranny of Colorado.

Slocum rode down into the smoke and dust to find
Pueblo's main street. Now that he was here, he had no
idea where to begin hunting for Esther Atkinson. Somehow, by not worrying too much about it and letting himself drift, he found himself heading for the rail yard. The
rattle of trains heading north and south deafened him,
making him wish for the high country again. But he resolutely crossed and recrossed the tracks, keeping an eagle
eye out for any trace of the vanished woman.

When he didn't see her, he dismounted and went into
the stationmaster's house. The man was reading the *Rocky
Mountain News* from the day before. He put down the
paper as Slocum walked in.

"Howdy, mister. What kin I do for you?"

"I'm looking for a young woman—"

The stationmaster's attitude hardened. "You want a whore, you git on down to the dance halls over on Elm Street."

"No, no, it's not like that. This one's been kidnapped, and her father sent me to find her."

"You look kinda familiar," the man said, squinting. "Have I seen you before?"

"Abel Stine hired me. I work for Clarence Atkinson."

"You hunting for *his* young'n?" The man's eyebrows arched and wiggled like furry caterpillars. He let out a laugh that echoed through the small room. "Tryin' to corral that filly is work no single man ought to be forced to do. She'll ride you and rope you and brand you and then move on—all in a single day."

"You've seen Esther Atkinson?" Slocum asked. "Within the past few days?"

"Reckon I have. She was with some galoot I never saw around here before. He wasn't a railroader, not from the way he was dressed. Had the same look as . . . you." The stationmaster looked to the worn ebony butt of Slocum's Colt Navy. "Might have been a gunfighter by trade."

"I'm no gunman," Slocum said. He saw the stationmaster wasn't inclined to believe him. "Where'd you see them together?"

"They was laughin' and carryin' on over at Miss Matilda's Café. 'Bout the best steaks in town there. She knows how to cook 'em jist right and—"

"When did you see Miss Atkinson there?" Slocum pressed.

"She didn't have the look of a woman bein' drug off ag'in her will," the man said. Slocum's gaze pinned him like a bug on a needle, and he seemed to shrink in on himself. "This mornin'," he said. " 'Bout breakfast time or a little later."

"Thanks," Slocum said. "If this pans out and there's a reward, I'll see you get a share."

"Why that's mighty neighborly of you. You might try the boardin'house jist 'cross the street from Miss Matilda's. If a lady's gonna stay in Pueblo, she can't do much better 'n there."

Slocum left in a hurry. This was the first substantial lead he'd had since beginning the hunt for Esther. He rode into town, asked for the café and found it. His belly growled, reminding him it had been a while since he'd eaten. He ordered a steak and fried potatoes with onions and found it to be everything the stationmaster had claimed. Forcing himself to eat slowly, Slocum watched the customers in the café and the boardinghouse entrance across the street. There wasn't much traffic, and he doubted he missed anyone coming or going from the house.

After a second helping of peach cobbler, Slocum was stuffed and ready to renew his search for Esther. He felt in his bones he was close. Walking across the street, he knocked on the door and waited until an older woman, her hair tied up in a rag, showing she had been dusting, answered.

"What can I do for you?" she asked, eyeing him from head to toe and obviously not liking what she saw.

"I have a message for Miss Atkinson," Slocum said. "From her mother."

"Atkinson? I have no one boarding here by that name." She slammed the door in his face. Slocum shrugged it off. Perhaps Esther wasn't here. All the stationmaster had said was this was a possibility and that he had only been sure of seeing her in the café.

Slocum looked up and down the street and was about to mount his horse and hunt elsewhere when he heard a familiar voice floating on the evening stillness.

Esther.

He left his horse tethered in front of the boardinghouse

and walked briskly down the street until he came to a
dance hall. Peering in, he saw a half dozen women, some
almost naked, dancing with steelworkers for a dime a
dance. Some left to go upstairs to the cribs. Others were
content with only feeling a woman pressing close for the
duration of a fast polka or a clumsy waltz.

In the rear, sitting between two men, was Esther Atkinson. She laughed and joked and drank as heavily as
any of the men. If she had been kidnapped, she was enjoying her captivity more than Slocum would have
thought possible. He pushed into the noisy dance hall and
made his way to the bar. Somewhere along the way, Esther spotted him. She and the young man with her stood
so fast they knocked over their chairs.

"Esther!" he called. She bolted for the rear of the saloon, the man following on her heels. Slocum lit out after
them, only to find his way blocked by the other man
who'd been with them.

"Where you g-goin'?" growled the hulking man.

Slocum had several choices. He could blow a hole in
the man's belly. That might be easier than trying to pound
his way through. The man had the look of granite about
him, as immovable as any mountain. Slocum realized
starting a gunfight in this saloon would only bring the
marshal and a herd of deputies down on his head.

"I want to see Esther," he said, shifting his weight to
the right. The man moved to block his way and Slocum
moved like lightning. His knee came up. Combined with
the movement the man initiated himself, the impact of
knee into groin doubled the man and sent him to the floor
with only a dull gasp of pain coming from his lips.

Slocum stepped over him and went into the alley behind the dance hall. Two whores worked to strip one of
their drunken victims. One woman snarled at him like
some feral beast. Slocum turned the other way in time to
see Esther and the man with her riding off in a buggy.

He ran to the end of the alley and stopped in the middle of the street, cursing his bad luck. By the time he returned to the boardinghouse and got his horse, there was no trace of Esther or the man with her.

"A buggy can't just vanish," he told himself. Instincts told him they were likely to show up again soon. If he went off half-cocked and tore about Pueblo looking for them, he wasn't likely to ever find them. Instead, he tied his paint to a hitching post and then he went to sit in a wooden chair at the corner of the boardwalk in front of the dance hall. Rocking back, Slocum pulled down his hat and enjoyed what passed for an evening breeze kicking up dust in the middle of the street.

His nose wrinkled at the odors coming to him. Something big had died and was decaying nearby. The stench from the industries made his eyes water, and the laughter from within the dance hall was a powerful magnet pulling at him. It had been too long since he'd tried a shot of whiskey.

But he endured, he fought down the call of demon rum, and he was rewarded. Less than twenty minutes after he'd started his vigil, he saw the buggy rattling to a halt in front of the saloon. It had come from the opposite direction, as if the driver had made a wide circle around town and had finally reckoned Slocum would be long gone.

The man jumped to the street, then reached out to help Esther down. She wasn't being held against her will, the best Slocum could see. But that didn't matter. Her mother and father wanted her back in the railroad camp.

"Esther," he said, walking up. "It's time to go."

"John!" she cried out in surprise. "I thought you—inside—there was—" The lovely young woman was taken aback and lost her senses for a moment.

"What do you want, mister?" the man with her said, interposing himself between Slocum and the girl.

Slocum eyed him and came to a quick decision. A

young buck who thought he was cock of the walk. There
was a nervousness about him that showed he had not been
in many, if any, gunfights. But one day he would. Slocum
wanted that day to be sometime in the future. All he was
interested in was returning Esther to her parents.

"This is between Miss Atkinson and me," Slocum said.

"No, it's between you 'n me," the would-be gunman
said. He pushed Esther back, then placed his right hand
against the holster dangling at his right hip.

"You don't want to do this," Slocum said. He heard the
music inside the dance hall stop. A hush fell over the revelers as they rushed to the windows and doors to see who
would die. A few placed bets. They all went against the
young gunman until the odds were too high for any gambler.

"They don't think you've got the grit," Slocum said.
"She's not worth dying over."

"Why, you!" Even as he spoke, the man went for his gun.

He was fast, very fast. Slocum was faster. His hand
was a blur as he drew his Colt Navy from the cross-draw
holster, cocked the single action and fired, almost at point-
blank range. The wadding and unburnt gunpowder from
the round set fire to the gunman's shirt even as the bullet
ripped through his gut and blasted his spine.

The man twitched, still standing upright, dropped his
gun from nerveless fingers, then collapsed, dead long before he hit the ground.

Slocum looked over at Esther. Her brown eyes were
big as saucers and her hand covered her mouth.

She made tiny mewling sounds like a stepped-on kitten.
Then she found her tongue.

"You killed him, John. You killed him!" She dropped
to the ground and cradled the man's head in her lap.

Slocum couldn't tell if tears were shed because he was
busy dealing with the law and trying to keep one eye on
Esther so she wouldn't run off again.

9

Slocum glanced over at Esther Atkinson. She rode her horse with her wide brown eyes straight ahead and had not said a word since they had ridden out of Pueblo. She had dried her tears and after that had shown no sign of emotion. It was as if she no longer cared about anything in the world, but Slocum had the feeling more that resignation possessed the young woman. Slocum had enough witnesses to the gunfight for the law to call it a killing in self-defense, but he felt as if it had been murder. Esther had relied too much on the young gunman, and he had been puffed up to defend her.

He'd never had a chance against someone as fast and accurate as John Slocum. In Slocum's mind that made his killing murder. It had been too easy.

But riding in silence wasn't. He had a thousand questions he wanted Esther to answer, and it was obvious she was not going to talk to him. Whether it came from sulking over being caught or not wanting to confess all she had done, he did not know. He thought it might be a little of both reasons.

"Ahead," Slocum said, pointing at the canyon stretching in front of them. He had followed the Colorado and

New Mexico tracks to the canyon where the bridge had been blown up. To his surprise, Abel Stine's workmen had rebuilt the structure. It was a little on the rickety side, but serviceable for two people walking their horses across.

From the Pueblo side of the canyon, Slocum dismounted and shouted across to Stine.

"Is the bridge safe? Looks like a good gust of wind will knock it down."

Stine didn't answer. He stepped out onto the bridge and walked across, expertly picking the right places to step. He quickly joined Slocum and Esther.

"Miss Esther!" Stine said, beaming. He was genuinely happy to see her safe and sound. "Slocum said he'd rescue you, and he's a man of his word. It's good to see you again." He looked as if he might hug her, but Esther shied away. Stine was grimy from work and smelled like a goat.

"Should I head to the west and skirt the bridge or do you think we can get across on it? Looks might chancy to me," Slocum said. He didn't cotton much to having the trestle collapse under him. Again.

"We salvaged most of the timber, so rebuilding went faster than I'd thought it would. We got track across in a hurry, but it won't hold an engine yet. But people? You can walk on it all day, and it'll never notice. We'll have it trussed up by tomorrow noon so it'll hold any narrow gauge engine in Colorado."

"I'm not sure Miss Atkinson is up to walking across," Slocum said, glancing in her direction. She looked hesitant but said nothing. He wasn't certain he wanted to try it, but going west to skirt the canyon would add a day or two getting back to camp. He was increasingly disgusted with Esther Atkinson, her father, and anything having to do with building railroads to nowhere through mountains.

"I'll get a handcar. We can hook on a small freight wagon and put your horses in that, then pump across the bridge."

"Let's do it a bit at a time," Slocum suggested. "People first, horses later."

Stine laughed. "It's good to see you both." He slapped Slocum on the shoulder and started back across the bridge to get the handcar.

"You have to do this, don't you, John?" asked Esther, speaking for the first time in hours and hours. All she had said before was when she needed to stop to relieve herself.

"It's what I'm hired to do," he said. "What—" He never got the chance to ask her what had happened because Stine returned, and Esther clamped her mouth shut and looked resolutely stolid again.

Slocum shrugged it off. He had done his job. As far as he was concerned, Henrietta Atkinson had already paid him for it. Taking part in a war between Atkinson and Villalobos wasn't in the cards for him since there could be no winners. Still, he wondered what was spurring the trouble. Murder, kidnapping, sabotage, and the source of it didn't seem to be in either camp.

"We're ridin' high now, folks," Stine said, pumping furiously to get them back to camp. His crew had a second handcar with the promised cargo hauler they'd use to get the horses across the canyon. "Your pa's gonna be so happy to see you, Miss Esther, he's sure to pop his buttons."

Esther stood on the front of the handcar, out of the way, when Slocum added his muscle to the pumping. The sooner they got to camp, the sooner he could head west. He wasn't certain where he wanted to go, but anywhere was fine as long as it was away.

Still, nagging questions ate at him. He wanted to hear what Esther told her parents about the kidnapping. There had not been a ransom demand and, if her abductors had intended to get back at Clarence Atkinson, she would have ended up dead, like Paco Villalobos.

A cheer went up from the half of the crew still in the

camp. Slocum was amazed at the progress made building the bridge across Cutthroat Gorge in his absence. Stine was a miracle worker in keeping the crews busy and productive. Unlike Carlos Villalobos, Atkinson took little part in the design or construction of the road, leaving it all to his capable foreman. Slocum hoped Stine got paid handsomely for his work. He deserved every penny and more.

"My dear! You're safe!" cried Clarence Atkinson. He jumped to the ground and let Esther run to him. She buried her face in his shoulder and began crying.

"Oh, Papa, it was terrible. Those men! Those awful, awful men took me away!"

"It's all right. I got you back. They didn't . . . hurt you, did they? If they did, I—"

"No, Papa, they didn't. It was such an ordeal. It's a wonder I managed to survive, but I did. Truly, I did."

She gushed on about how dreadful it had been for her. Slocum wanted to tell her father the situation when he had found her. Esther didn't seem too frightened in the company of the young gunfighter. If anything, she had been living it up.

Slocum started to speak up, but Esther turned to him and gave him a lewd wink. She mouthed out, "Tonight. My car," and then winked again at him to let him know what his reward would be for keeping silent about her escapades.

If Slocum had been uncertain about all that had happened, this cleared up everything for him. Esther hadn't been kidnapped, but had run off with the young gunman. How she had contacted him or when they'd made the plans for her to sneak off, he neither knew nor cared. She had put her mother through needless worry to go off on a lark.

Clarence Atkinson and his daughter went up into the railroad magnate's car. Slocum started to go to Henrietta's to let the woman know her daughter was safe, but Abel Stine called out to him.

"Slocum, hold your horses. Don't go runnin' off yet. Here's something for you." The foreman held out a thick wad of greenbacks.

"What's that?"

"Your reward," Stine said. "Mr. Atkinson authorized a reward of five hundred dollars for returning Miss Esther safe and sound. You did that, so the money's yours."

Slocum took it, folded it into a thick wad, and stuffed the bills into his shirt pocket. He had gotten paid well for returning the wayward railroad heiress. If he stayed in camp until after everyone else had gone to bed, he could collect another reward from Esther for not revealing all that had really happened. He could win twice.

Success tasted like ash in his mouth.

"You be needing me anymore?" Slocum asked, thinking it was time for him to ride on. "I'll buy the paint from you. He's a sturdy enough horse and handles mountain trails as surefooted as a burro."

"Well, we got some problems around here I want you to look into. You done such a fine job fetching back Miss Esther, I thought you could help out finding who is sabotaging the track."

"Villalobos?" Slocum guessed.

"Probably his man, but I suspect someone in the camp. Don't know who since most of the men have been with me for months and months. I thought I could trust the whole scurvy lot of them. Reckon that's not so."

"You've about got the bridge rebuilt. Any trouble there?" Slocum saw the expression on Stine's face. There was more to the request than finding a traitor in Atkinson's work crew.

"It's like this. I think whoever's been burning our ties and pushing our rail down into gullies so we have to go and lug it back is gettin' orders from outside."

"Pueblo?" Slocum guessed.

"You must be a mind reader," Stine said, eyeing him warily. "How'd you guess that?"

Slocum shrugged it off. "I see things. Villalobos is having the same trouble you are."

"We're not doin' it to him!" protested Stine.

"And he'd say the same about the source of your troubles," Slocum countered. "Might be you are both right."

"I don't understand."

"I'll get back to Pueblo and poke around. By the time I find out anything, you ought to have the bridge repaired and be able to send a train into town."

"It'll be Mr. Atkinson's personal engine. It's the only one we have working right now."

"Good enough," Slocum said. "I'll report back in a week or so." With that, he mounted his paint and started back down the tracks toward the bridge. The horse shied repeatedly, knowing it had to recross the bridge in the bed of the cargo hauler. Slocum kept it under control, as well as his own uneasiness, as the handcar pumped across the bridge and over the sheer drop that had ended the lives of so many men.

Slocum was tired not in body, but in spirit by the time he reached Pueblo again. He seemed to be retracing old paths, hunting for new spoor. That seldom worked, but he had no other choice. The only thing different this time was tracking down the identity of the man who had been squiring around Esther Atkinson. Find out who he had been and Slocum figured he could determine what was going on out at the railroad construction camp.

Esther was mixed up in some kind of illicit scheme, one that did not include her father. Or her mother. What it might be he was not certain, but he wanted to find out and then clear out of Colorado entirely.

He started at the dance hall where he had shot and

killed the young buck. As he walked in, all eyes turned and a whisper passed through the crowd. They still recognized him. He bellied up to the bar, surprised to find the barkeep had already set him with a shot of red-eye whiskey.

"You want anything else, you let me know," the man said. "On the house. Anything you want."

"Don't see many men gunned down, do you?" Slocum asked.

The man smiled weakly and said, "Not really. This is a rough and tumble town, but the men working in the mills use their fists. Saw a man beat to death once. Messy as hell. But that was the first man I ever saw shot to death."

"Who was he? The marshal didn't seem to have a name for him when I left with the woman he had kidnapped."

"Kidnapped? The pair of them, along with Stuttering Dave, was in here all the time together, laughin' and carryin' on. Life was nothin' but a big party for them. Free spenders, too, the trio."

"Stuttering Dave still around?" Slocum asked. He had forgotten about the giant of a man he had laid out before going after Esther and her escort.

"Sure. He's sweet on Molly, that one back there. She takes every dime he has, poor sucker. But I haven't seen Dave today."

"Then I reckon I'll wait." Slocum took a half bottle of rotgut and settled down in a chair by the door where he could watch everything going on in the dance hall. Molly was a skinny but popular woman, maybe in her forties, possibly only rode-hard-and-put-away-wet twenties. But when the men swarming around her like flies began to buzz away, Slocum perked up.

Stuttering Dave came in, a broad grin on his ugly face. He went straight to her and settled down. Molly started to say something to him, saw Slocum coming over, and then turned and hightailed it up the stairs to the cribs.

"M-molly, w-wait. W-why you r-runnin' like that?" Dave got out.

Slocum drew his pistol, cocked it by Stuttering Dave's ear, and pressed the cold muzzle into the man's temple.

"I have a couple questions. Answer, and you'll be upstairs in Molly's bed before you know it."

"I . . . I don't know n-nuthin', m-mister," he got out.

"Let's start with your partner's name."

"K-kid C-calico," he got out. For a moment Slocum considered squeezing the trigger because he thought Dave was funning him. Then he realized the trouble came from the dead would-be gunman and not Stuttering Dave.

"Kid Calico," he said, wondering if this was some greenhorn from back East who had read too many dime novels. "He's dead. The two of you worked for . . . ?" He prodded the man with his gun. From behind Slocum heard chair legs scraping across the wood floor as men vacated the premises. If shooting started again, they didn't want to end up dead like Kid Calico.

"The g-general."

"Who?"

"G-general Palmer. Thass who he s-said we was w-workin' for."

"What about Esther Atkinson?"

"Who?"

"The woman with you," Slocum said, getting mad now. "That was Clarence Atkinson's daughter."

"Who's h-he?"

"What name did she use?"

"Rita. She s-said her na-name was Rita."

"So you and the Kid worked for General Palmer. The same man who owns the Denver and Rio Grande railroad?"

"Y-yes. But with the K-kid dead, I don't get no more m-money. He was the one who p-paid me."

Slocum was beginning to get the picture now, but he had to be certain. General William J. Palmer was the Colorado pioneer at putting in narrow-gauge track to places even a mountain goat thought twice about venturing. He had become fabulously wealthy and had even started a regular-gauge line from Denver to Salt Lake City, in direct competition with Jay Gould's Union Pacific line. The more Slocum unearthed, the more he thought Villalobos and Atkinson were mere pawns in a bigger game.

But who were the real players? And how did Esther Atkinson fit into the picture? He shook his head. There wasn't any picture forming, just broken pieces that had to be fitted together. He was not sure he even had all the pieces yet, but it felt close this time. Really close.

"Here's five dollars," he said, dropping a bill onto the table in front of Stuttering Dave. "Why don't you go see how much you can get from Molly for it."

"Th-thanks, m-mister," said the man, snatching up the bill and clutching it in his hand.

Slocum holstered his hogleg and went to find his horse. It was a long ride to Manitou Springs and the headquarters for the General's D&RG Railroad.

10

After passing through the peculiarly colored, wind-carved grotesque rocks in what the Arapaho called the Garden of the Gods, Slocum turned his paint westward up into the mountains, following the snaky road to Manitou Springs. To one side of the road ran a narrow-gauge railroad track leading from Colorado Springs back to General Palmer's personal retreat in the foothills. There wasn't much traffic along the road; Slocum thought this was due to the D&RG making adequate numbers of trips in and out. But one strange thing drew his full attention. Sulfur smells made his nose wrinkle and on both sides of the road stretched elaborate, posh, hot springs spas named after Indian tribes.

Slocum had never understood what people got out of bathing in the hot, stinking waters, but the signs along the road advertised amazing therapeutic benefits. The flashy hotels and expensive spas were filled with people from back East, if Slocum read their clothing styles right. Many were certainly not from Denver or even St. Louis from the way they talked, walked, and wandered about commenting on the towering mountains and the fineness of the healing waters.

"Mister, sell you a bottle o' water. Only two dollars,"

called a barker at a wooden stand with a crudely painted sign alongside the road. "Comes from Navajo Springs, and it'll cure what ails ya!" The man held up a bottle of murky water.

Slocum wasn't sure what ailed him, but drinking the bitter water wasn't likely to do it. He preferred a decent saloon where he could get a shot of whiskey to take the trail dust out of his throat. He rode on, finding himself plunging deeper and deeper into the retreat of the truly rich. Buggy drivers genteelly snapped whips to get well-groomed horses a'prancing for the bored-looking passengers on their way to yet another mineral bath. On the hill overlooking the main road was a fabulous four-story hotel. Drifting down and forcing away the sharp sulfur smell from the springs were cooking odors that made Slocum's mouth water.

He touched his shirt pocket. He had most of the reward money Stine had given him for taking Esther back to her parents. He could afford any meal. Then he looked down at his dirty, trail-worn clothing and knew they would never let him into the lobby, much less the dining room for a seven-course meal.

He kept riding until he found a spot a mile past the four-story hotel to camp. The water coming out of the ground and bubbling into a pool carried the faint sulfur taste of all water burbling up around Manitou Springs, but Slocum didn't mind. And it did not cost $2 for an amount hardly capable of wetting his whistle.

Something alerted him to trouble. He sat up and looked around. Nothing. The sense of being watched grew stronger. Slocum slipped off the leather thong holding his six-shooter in its holster.

"Wouldn't consider drawing that piece of iron, if I were you, pardner," came a slow drawl.

Slocum looked over his shoulder. Somehow a man had

perched on the rocks above him, and he had not heard him until he spoke.

"I reckon a man like you's wonderin' how I did it," the well-dressed man said. He pushed back his coat to let the sun catch the silver marshal's badge pinned to his vest. "Fact is, I was raised by the Cheyenne. Never saw a better bunch of trackers, and they could walk right up to a cavalry trooper without him ever knowing and steal his false teeth right from his mouth."

"Good thing I don't have china clippers," Slocum said.

"Good thing you take advice." The marshal gestured and from three different locations appeared deputies, all with rifles trained on Slocum. "These boys didn't just grow up with the Cheyenne. They *are* Cheyenne."

"Unusual to have so many Indians sworn in as deputies."

"Folks in these parts care more about keepin' the peace than they do anything else. They wouldn't much care if all my boys carried pitchforks and had horns and spade-tipped tails."

"The brimstone smell is all around," Slocum said, wondering where the conversation was heading. He felt chagrined that the marshal had managed to not only sneak up on him, but bring in three deputies without ever revealing themselves.

The marshal laughed. "It's good you see the humor in it because I've got to ask you some hard questions. What the hell are you doin' in my valley?"

The light tone had turned into razor-edged questioning.

"I'm here on some business for Clarence Atkinson," Slocum said, figuring this wasn't far from the truth. "His daughter was kidnapped. I'm trying to find out who was responsible."

"Never heard 'bout this."

"She's back with her family now," Slocum said.

"You responsible for rescuing her? How'd that come about?"

"I shot the man who was holding her. Over in Pueblo."

"Tough town, Pueblo," the marshal said. "Not like Manitou Springs. We're real law-abidin' here, and I intend to keep it that way."

"My sources tell me General Palmer might know something about the men who were holding Miss Atkinson."

"Doubt that. Even if it was true, I couldn't let you bother the General. He's not only a busy man, he's an important one in these parts. Without him and his railroad, Manitou Springs might not exist."

"DR and G coming in here from Denver?"

"You got it, mister," said the marshal. "He brings in five trainloads of tourists and health seekers a week. Without them, this place would dry up and blow away."

"I see you have an investment to protect. I'm not here to cause trouble, just get some answers."

"Might be the same thing," observed the marshal. "What's the name of the galoot you caught with Atkinson's daughter?"

"His partner, a man named stuttering Dave, called him Kid Calico."

The marshal laughed. "Him? I remember him. I run him out of town a couple months ago. A blowhard who fancied himself a killer, but I suspect he never had drawn his six-gun on another man."

"About the way I saw it," Slocum said. He remembered how easy it had been to kill Kid Calico. It was him or Slocum, but the death still didn't set well with him.

"He might have worked for the General once, but holding a job when you're such an arrogant snot is hard," the marshal said. He gestured and sent his deputies fading back into the landscape where they'd come from. Slocum appreciated the skill with which they moved. Even watching them, it was hard to see where they went. They walked on silent feet and probably didn't give a tracker much to follow in the way of a trail, either.

"Mind if I inquire after Kid Calico?"

"Do it, but be out of Manitou Springs by tomorrow noon. And don't go botherin' the General. Check with his agent at the Hot Springs Hotel. If he don't tell you anythin', then you clear out right away. That suit you?" The marshal stared down at Slocum, hand resting on the butt of his six-shooter in its holster.

"Suits me," Slocum said, knowing it when a man told him to get out of town—or else. This marshal was one tough hombre whom Slocum didn't want to cross.

He dismounted and went looking for the Hot Springs Hotel, finding it another mile up the road. The scent of sulfur was stronger near the hotel. Slocum saw a half dozen shallow, bubbling pools and the yellowish crystal-caked rims around them. Guests soaked in the water, gaining therapeutic benefits he couldn't quite understand. To get even more healing, they choked down the bitter water by the quart.

Dismounting in front of the posh hotel, Slocum went up to the front porch. A liveried servant blocked his way into the lobby, eyeing him from head to foot.

"I'm here to talk to General Palmer's agent. The marshal said it was all right."

"Indeed," said the doorman, a slight hint of British accent carrying nothing but condescension with it. "I shall see. There," he said, pointing to chairs at the far back of the porch.

Slocum sat in the chair, staring out into the steep valley holding Manitou Springs. It was a spread-out town, mostly resort hotels and places catering to visitors from back East and all over the world. Not the kind of town he was comfortable in. From inside the hotel came dance music and the sound of guests enjoying themselves at some grand cotillion. The smell of cooking food overwhelmed—almost—the stench of sulfur from the springs and made Slocum's mouth water.

He forgot his hunger when a man strode up to him.

"You want something?" the man said brusquely.

"Kid Calico and his partner, Stuttering Dave. What can you tell me about them?"

For a moment the man's face took on a puzzled look, then a small grin curled his lips. "Dave I remember. Kid Calico? You might mean Horace Smith, a young buck who thought he was a lot tougher than he really was."

"That might be him." Slocum barely began describing Kid Calico when the man held up his hand for him to stop.

"He's the one. I fired him for malingering, him and Dave Slausen, the one with the stutter. Don't rightly know where he went, but there was a rumor he went to work for the Tall Pines Railroad Company."

"What's that? Never heard of them," said Slocum.

"Some upstart company from Denver. The General said not to worry my head over them and I haven't. Don't even know who's financing them, but if they hire men like Smith and Slausen, they've taken on more trouble than they can handle."

"Thanks," Slocum said. He heard the gaiety within and again smelled the food being prepared for the gala. Remembering the marshal's warning put him back into the saddle and riding out of the valley, leaving behind Manitou Springs as he headed north to Denver.

He should have taken the train to Denver. The road was long and dusty, and Slocum was so tired he was falling asleep in the saddle by the time he crossed Cherry Creek and went down into the heart of Denver. It had been less than three weeks since he had been here and had been bested by Abel Stine in the card game, but the town seemed alien now and a thousand years off in time.

He crossed the ribbons of railroad track and made his way to the stationmaster's office. Poking his head into the office, he called out, "Anyone here?"

No answer.

Trains came and went constantly through the hub of steel rails and not finding the man responsible for guiding the cargo in and out and through the maze was strange.

He went in and looked around, spotting a note on the desk: Gone to Lunch.

Slocum snorted in disgust. It was almost four in the afternoon. That was a powerful long lunch. Stepping outside he saw a man with holes burned in his clothing from being too close to too many hot cinders.

"Hey, mister," Slocum shouted. "Where do I find the stationmaster? I need to ask him about the Tall Pines railroad."

"Add's taking a break," the man said, peering nearsightedly at Slocum. "Who are you and what do you want with him?" The man squinted a little harder. Before he came too close Slocum answered.

"I've been talking to General Palmer about the way this yard's run. Him and Mr. Gould are thinking of making some changes. I need to talk to Add about it."

"Golly," the man said, looking like a rabbit ready to bolt for its burrow. "I didn't know anyone official was comin'."

"What's the stationmaster's full name?" Slocum asked.

"Why, Adam Claridge. He's a good man, but prone to not spend much time on the job. Don't hold that ag'in him now, now will you?"

"I'll talk to Mr. Gould about it," Slocum said, mounting. "Where'm I most likely to find Add right now. Some saloon?"

"The Fourflusher a couple hunnerd yards that away." The man squinted and pointed, then changed direction as if unsure where the saloon might be.

"I'll let the boss know you helped me out. Who knows? You might be the next stationmaster."

"Think so? Anything you need," the man shouted after Slocum, "jist ask!"

In spite of the ambiguous directions, finding the saloon wasn't hard, nor was finding the drunken stationmaster. The man was hardly able to sit in his chair. Two men held him upright as they rummaged through his pockets. Slocum didn't stop them from stealing Add Claridge's money, but he drew then line when they started to take his railroad watch.

The two looked up, eyes wide when Slocum towered over them.

"What you want?" growled one.

"Put the watch back. Keep the money but vamoose. Mr. Claridge and I have some business, and it doesn't concern you."

The two exchanged a quick glance, then faded into the crowd filling the Fourflusher. Slocum dropped into one of the now empty chairs beside the stationmaster.

"You wanna drink?" Add almost fell from the chair from the effort of speaking. Slocum grabbed him and pulled him back.

"Tell me about Horace Smith and Dave Slausen. They worked for the Tall Pines railroad."

"Smith? Slausen?" Add Claridge mangled the names, slurring from too much booze. Slocum motioned for the barkeep to bring over another bottle. Since the two sneak thieves had emptied the stationmaster's pockets, Claridge wasn't likely to pay for his own tarantula juice.

"Drink up. On me," Slocum said, pouring the man a shot. Add Claridge knocked it back. For a moment, Slocum thought it had knocked him out. Instead, the stationmaster's eyes cleared a little, and he focused more on what went on around him. "Needed that," he said.

"You know those two?"

"Nope, can't say I do, but the goldarned Tall Pines railroad, now, thass s-something else." He hiccuped. Slocum poured another drink, wondering what the man's tolerance was. One or two shots might bring him around, but there had to be a limit beyond which Add simply passed out.

"What about the railroad?" Slocum coaxed.

"S-strange goings-on, if you ast me," Add said. "Next door to this very establishment. Never anybody in their offices. I come up to get some money but no one's there. Been waitin', too, too long." Adam Claridge collapsed onto the table dead drunk.

Slocum took a swig of the whiskey, then put the bottle down on the table. He quickly left the saloon and checked the east side of the building, finding an empty lot. On the west side was a bank. He wondered if the stationmaster had been too much in his cups to know what he was saying. Then Slocum spied the crudely hand-lettered sign in the window of the storefront across the street from the saloon.

"So that's the headquarters for the Tall Pines railroad," he said. It took him only a few seconds to find what it had taken the stationmaster all afternoon to discover. The office was closed up tighter than a drum. Slocum went to the back, boldly walked down the alley, and gripped the doorknob. Locked. But not for long. It yielded under his strong twisting until it broke off, and the door opened on squeaky hinges. Slocum wasted no time getting out of the alley and into the railroad offices.

"Add Claridge, you're one smart fellow," Slocum said. There was a lot of dust around what appeared to be an abandoned office, except for the sign in the window and a solitary desk and chair up by the window. Behind it stood a low cabinet, its door chained shut.

This was too enticing for Slocum to pass up. If he wanted to find out all he could of Kid Calico and Stuttering Dave—not to mention possibly getting a clue about Esther Atkinson's kidnapping—the only place to look was in the cabinet. The lock was new and shiny and out of place with the rest of the furniture in the dirty office.

Slocum checked the desk for something to use to pry open the cabinet or break the lock. As he drew open the slim, center drawer he found a map covered with red and blue marks. He sat in the chair and stared at the map, trying to figure out what it meant. Slowly tracing the Colorado and New Mexico railroad route marked in blue, he saw where it went into Pueblo. Likewise, the heavy black lines were those established by Carlos Villalobos and his Colorado Southern.

The Denver and Rio Grande was in green and the Union Pacific in a chalky white, as if it did not matter. The four roads formed a curious spider pattern that seemed unrelated until Slocum saw how the red lines—those representing the Tall Pines railroad—connected the others. By itself, the Tall Pines held only worthless routes of little commercial value. Tied in with those of Atkinson and Villalobos, it surrounded General Palmer's D&RG, making it a rival to Jay Gould's more extensive Union Pacific line.

"Drive out Villalobos and Atkinson and take over those lines and the entire state of Colorado falls to whoever owns the Tall Pines railroad," Slocum said softly. He looked over his shoulder at the locked cabinet again. The owner of the road might just be the one behind the sabotage on both Villalobos's and Atkinson's railroads, not to mention Paco Villalobos's murder and Esther's kidnapping.

It was an ambitious plan and one that might require murder and kidnapping along with the sabotage. Slocum heaved a sigh, closed the drawer with the map in it, and turned his attention to opening the locked cabinet.

He fingered the lock, wondering if he ought to simply

shoot it off. Slocum had tried that before and had been wounded in the leg when a piece of lead had ricocheted off the lock and hit him. Still, it was the fastest way to open the cabinet and find out what lay within.

Drawing his six-shooter, he stepped back and aimed. Then he hesitated. The sound of squeaking floorboards and boots grinding into dust and grit came to him. And the man wearing those boots was trying to walk silently. Slocum spun, aimed, and fired toward the rear of the office. He was rewarded with a loud yelp of pain. The curses that followed told him he had only winged the man, not put him down for good.

Then Slocum was forced behind the desk as his assailant opened fire. He ducked about the side of the desk, trying to get a glimpse of the man for another shot. Instead of seeing his enemy, Slocum felt a sharp pain that lanced all the way up into his shoulder from his forearm. He shifted his weight and clutched at his right arm where the bullet had cut a deep furrow into his flesh.

Even after only a few seconds his hand was turning cold and numb. The six-gun slipped from his fingers to the floor with a heavy crash. Awkwardly grabbing it with his left hand, he got off a shot in the direction of the other gunman, just to keep him under cover.

Slocum felt a little woozy from his wound. What had felt cold at first now burned like a million wasps had chosen his flesh for their nest. The pain never slackened, and his right arm hung limp at his side. Poking his head above the desk, then ducking back, brought a trio of slugs whistling through the air for his face.

Another feint, another shot fired, then Slocum ran for the front door, firing clumsily as he went. He crashed into the wall, bounced back, shoved his Colt Navy into its holster and used his left hand to draw open the bolt locking the door. Another shot missed him, then he heard the other man's six-shooter click on an empty chamber.

This gave Slocum the chance to get through the front door and stumble into the street between the office and the Fourflusher saloon. Although he had a couple rounds left in his own pistol and he wanted to see who it was shooting at him, he knew this wasn't the right time to press the fight. If the man inside the Tall Pines railroad was honest, he'd call the Denver police to come arrest Slocum. And if he wasn't, he would cut him down where he stood given half a chance. In his current condition, Slocum didn't think he was up to waging any fight with an unknown gunman to open what may have been an empty—or innocent—cabinet.

He wasted no time making his getaway. Slocum didn't know what he might have found in the cabinet, but the map told him plenty.

It just didn't tell him who was behind the scheme to take over both Atkinson's and Villalobos's railroads.

11

"That's a nasty wound you got there," the doctor said, examining Slocum's arm. He held up the right arm and pulled it straight. Slocum winced in pain but said nothing. "Don't look much like you caught it on a nail."

"That's what happened," Slocum said, not wanting to explain how he'd gotten into a gunfight after breaking into the office of Tall Pines Railroad Company. It had taken twenty minutes before Slocum found the doctor in a saloon down the street, drinking a beer. Knowing nothing about the man other than he had a black bag and seemed sober enough to patch him up, Slocum had taken the chance the doctor could help. If the doctor got too suspicious, he might tell the police. Then Slocum would have a powerful lot of explaining to do. Breaking into the office would be the least of his worries if he was put in jail, where his unseen attacker could identify and maybe kill him.

Fish in a barrel, prisoner in a cell. Slocum shivered a little thinking how helpless he would be with a gimpy arm and no gun.

"This kind of wound used to show up all the time in these parts. Not so much anymore now that we got a good, reasonably honest police force patrolling the streets." The doctor set about cleaning the long bullet wound. "Don't suppose a man like you would want to admit being shot and robbed on the street, would you?"

"Don't think a man like me would want to admit a woman did this, either," Slocum said, saying the first thing that came into his head.

"As long as you weren't in a gunfight. The police don't like that one little bit. Bad for the city's image. Makes it seem like we're no better than some of the wilder boom-towns on the other side of the Front Range."

Slocum grimaced again as the doctor started suturing the wound, taking twenty stitches in a neat, precise row. He was glad this had happened in Denver instead of out in the mountains. He might have lost use of the arm to give a permanent reminder of how stupid he had been turning his back on an open doorway and not checking the premises for anyone else before tackling the locked cabinet. The office had seemed deserted, so he assumed it was entirely vacant. The man who had tried to bush-whack him must have been in an adjacent room, probably sleeping when he was supposed to be standing guard.

"Five dollars," the doctor said, snipping off the end of the suture with a pair of surgical scissors. "You'll be good as gold in a few days. Try not to put too much stress on that arm and eat a good porterhouse or two. That perks folks up and helps the healing. Here's the name of a good place to eat. You can tell the owner that Doc McKenzie sent you over. He'll be sure to give you the best in the house."

Slocum looked at the small handbill Doctor McKenzie pulled from his bag.

"My wife's brother runs it. He's a no account lowlife, but he fixes a mean steak. Stay away from the greens, though. Never could figure where he gets them."

"Thanks, Doctor." Slocum fumbled out the money and

paid the bill. He wondered if McKenzie might not go to the police to tell of a gunshot wound. There might even be bounties now that Denver called itself the "Queen City of the West" and tried to present a more civilized view to all the people from the East pouring through. He remembered the genteel society with their fancy dress and cotillions and sumptuous dining down in Manitou Springs and knew the marshal there thought the same.

Shoot off a gun and you'd be hustled out of town so fast your head would spin. Kill someone and the law would hang you high—and out of sight of the tourists.

Slocum awkwardly got his shirt on, vowing to look for another before he hit the trail. The blood had caked the parts of the right sleeve that weren't torn away by the bullet as it ran the entire length of his forearm. It was late, but he went by the office where the shoot-out had occurred. Slocum wanted to sneak back inside and see what the cabinet held, but a half dozen men prowled the building now, all looking alert and several carrying scatterguns. He had lost his chance for the night.

"Later," he said, but he knew that wouldn't happen. If there ever had been anything of importance in the cabinet, it would be removed. The only tidbit he had come up with was the map showing how the owner of Tall Pines Railroad intended circling and then devouring the lines of other, smaller builders.

Slocum didn't know how easy it would be to take over Atkinson or Villalobos, but General Palmer would be quite a mouthful to swallow. Still, with the other two roads firmly combined into one larger line, it was possible. Nothing less than railroad travel in a thriving, rich state was at stake.

He headed back toward the rail yard to see what more information he could unearth about the owner of Tall Pines Railroad when a loud voice froze him in his tracks.

"Slocum!"

He turned, knowing he could never get his six-shooter out without fumbling. Then Slocum relaxed. Abel Stine hurried to him.

"What are you doing in Denver?" Slocum asked.

"We got bad trouble," the foreman said, out of breath. "I brought Mr. Atkinson's locomotive into town to pick up supplies—and as many men as I could."

"We've been through this before," Slocum said tiredly. "You need workers, not gunfighters."

"They're killin' us as we work, John. Snipers. We've had a half dozen men seriously wounded. One was killed. Poor Paddy. Never had a chance. They shot him smack in the chest, and he toppled over like a cut tree. I saw it happen and couldn't do a thing. Couldn't even see where the damned owlhoot was that shot him."

"So what do you intend to do?" Slocum asked, knowing the answer from the set of Stine's jaw.

"Villalobos kills us, we do the same to him. I'm lookin' for men to be snipers."

"That's not a good idea," Slocum said. "If the army gets wind of this, they might send out soldiers. It looks more like a range war brewing than railroads building."

"Good, let them protect us while we work," Stine said. "I don't want anything but to build my road—Mr. Atkinson's road," he quickly corrected. "I can't do it if Villalobos kills all my men."

Slocum found himself tossed on the horns of a dilemma. He wanted no part in what was brewing down south in the mountains. This kind of war left nothing but dead men and hard feelings. It never ended to anyone's satisfaction. He ought to ride away, but felt some obligation to see this through, even if it got more bloody.

Rubbing his right arm, he knew it had almost been over for him.

"What about Mrs. Atkinson?" he asked. "And Miss Esther?"

"I brought them back here to Denver. They can stay here where it's safe."

"Not so safe if Villalobos wants to harm them," Slocum said. "Why not send them back East? Or on out to San Francisco? Somewhere out of the state."

"They'd never agree," said Stine. "Besides, the boss wants 'em safe, but not too far away."

Slocum could understand the man's thinking, even as he saw the danger. Without proper guards, the two women were in constant danger. His lips curled slightly as he thought of Esther Atkinson. Without a chain around her ankle, she might hightail it again and end up dealing with the devil once more.

"Don't fret over them. We need to worry about the killing going on down at the camp."

Slocum heaved a sigh. "Load my paint into a freight car, and let's get back down. Maybe I can do something to pull the fuse on this powder keg." Even as the words slipped past his lips, Slocum knew that possibility was slimmer than drawing to an inside straight. But what choice did he have?

"You think putting guards on those rocks will help?" Stine asked, frowning. "Don't look to be all that much help if they start shooting at us from over yonder."

"That's a two hundred yard shot. The sentries will see anyone creeping up on you long before they get within range," Slocum assured the foreman. "You tend to laying track and building the bridge, and I'll see to it you're left alone."

The look of relief told Slocum where Stine's heart lay. He was a railroader, and this shooting and killing was a distraction to his job. Stine was willing to let anyone else tend to security if he could work in peace.

The men guarding the workers weren't the best Slocum had seen, but they would do. Stine had recruited them out of the saloons in Larrimer Square, as he had the others who had died when the train crashed into the canyon.

"Let's see how you're doing with the bridge across Cutthroat Gorge," Slocum said. Shooting the workers was less on his mind than another bomb planted on the new railroad trestle. If Atkinson's personal locomotive was put out of commission, the C&NM would be out of business. Atkinson would have replaced the other engine by now if he'd had either the cash or the bank loans to do so. Every time the railroad magnate faced rearward from his car and saw his personal engine dragging along freight cars, it looked as if he had bitten into something sour and foul tasting.

But to build the line, Clarence Atkinson would sacrifice anything. His entire life was wrapped up in this venture, even if it meant not traveling in the style to which he had become accustomed.

Wind sliced at Slocum's face and made his eyes water when he stood at the brink of Cutthroat Gorge. The sheer walls fell fast to the river below, but the span was the shortest anywhere along the canyon, making this a good spot for a bridge. Carlos Villalobos had to span twice this distance up the canyon before he could get his railroad to the other side to service the rich mining camps there.

"What are you looking for?" asked Stine. "More dynamite?"

"Something like that. Don't see how anyone can approach the trestles by coming along the walls. They'd have to be down on the riverbank to plant another bomb. Put a couple guards down there, along with the crew," Slocum said.

"And?" Stine looked at him, his knit cap slipping up a little on his head. He tugged it back into place. "What else are you thinking?"

"You don't win a war building a fort and waiting to kill off anyone attacking you. It's time I went to Villalobos's camp to see what's going on there."

"You still don't think he's responsible for our troubles, do you?"

"Can't say for certain," Slocum admitted. He turned and covered his ear on the side of the incessant wind whistling through the gorge. "You hear something?"

"Shots!" cried Abel Stine.

Together, the foreman and Slocum ran back along the track to the camp. It was getting toward dusk, and here and there in the rocks stabbed dangerous, foot-long tongues of yellow-orange muzzle flash. The report and the whine of bullets bouncing off rocks filled the air. Worse, from around the camp came the moans of men struck by the flying lead.

"Keep down, let the armed men handle this!" shouted Slocum. He looked up into the rocks, wondering why the guards he had posted were not returning fire. A cold knot twisted his belly when he thought they might all be dead—or traitors. Stine had not asked for bona fides on any of the men he had hired. Villalobos could have placed them where Stine would be sure to find and hire them.

The barrage kept up as Slocum made his way from one post to another, finding the men Stine had hired were all cowering, fearful for their lives. Slocum shook them and got their attention.

"We're going to attack," he said. "You'll fire those rifles at the men killing everyone in camp. If you don't, I swear I'll shoot you myself." His cold tone convinced several of the men. One or two others looked skeptical. Slocum drew his six-shooter the best he could left-handed, cocked, and fired.

One man's hat went sailing into the darkness.

"Why'd you do that?" the man cried. "That was a new hat. I paid seven dollars for it!"

"I meant to blow off your damned head," Slocum said. "I'll do better next time unless you lead the attack against them." He gestured in the direction of the snipers still picking off easy targets in the camp.

"You or them?" the man said, swallowing hard.

"I've never missed with a second shot," Slocum assured him. The man levered a round into his rifle and spun around, tearing off toward the snipers and screaming at the top of his lungs. The rest with Slocum hesitated, then followed. He trailed them, knowing any shooting he did would be off target. In a day or two he might have use of his right arm back, but not now.

Like a band of wild Indians, the men rushed into the rocks and scaled the places where Slocum had thought no sniper could accurately fire from. To his surprise, the attack did not turn into a massacre. The snipers cried in fear, turned, and ran. He heard the pounding of their horses' hooves long before he had gained the top of the rocks where they had begun their all-too-accurate attack.

"We did it, we chased 'em off!" crowed the man Slocum had threatened.

"Get horses from the corral," Slocum said. "We're going after them."

"After them? Why? We ran 'em off."

"I want to see where they're headed." Slocum knew the killers had hightailed it in the direction of Villalobos's camp, but that meant nothing. The only other way to escape would have been back down the Colorado and New Mexico tracks.

"I'm comin' with you," Stine said, rifle clutched in his hand.

"You know how to use that thing?" Slocum asked.

Stine pulled back his knit cap. In the darkness it took Slocum a few seconds to understand what he was staring at. Abel Stine had been scalped and used the knit cap to cover up the scars where his hair had once been.

"Sioux," he said. "At Plum Creek when I was working on a road there. They killed everyone else and scalped

me, thinkin' I was dead. I learned to use a rifle. Not one
of them murderous savages is alive today. Yeah, Slocum,
I know how to use a rifle."

The foreman pulled the cap back down and went to
find a horse. Slocum shook his head. You never knew
about men.

He followed, his right arm giving him occasional
twinges of pain. Don't strain it, Doctor McKenzie had
said. The doctor hadn't known Slocum was going into the
jaws of hell.

"Everybody ready?" Slocum called, climbing onto his
paint. The horse neighed, as if wary of so much activity
this late in the day. Slocum motioned for them to follow
him as he set out to find the trail left by the bushwhackers.

Finding it was remarkably easy. Too easy. Following
was simple, too, every yard of the way. It was as if the
fleeing men had done all they could to lead any party after
them directly into Villalobos's camp.

"They *were* sent by Villalobos!" cried Stine. Even the
foreman figured out what the spoor meant. "We're gonna
give 'em what for, men. Into their camp and shoot it up,
just like they did ours!"

"No, wait!" Slocum called, but the blood lust had set
in. The need for revenge was too great. Slocum wondered
if Stine wasn't reliving the days of vengeance when he
had hunted down the Sioux responsible for so much death
and misery. Then he had other things to worry over.

The workers in Villalobos's camp had not been prepared for the onslaught, but they responded as well as
anyone outside an army bivouac might. Stine's attack
swept through the camp and came back like the ocean's
tide. The first pass had been unopposed. The second
turned bloody.

"Get out of here," cried Slocum. He managed to grab
Stine and shake him. The foreman almost fell from his
horse. Slocum saw two bullet holes in the man's side.

Neither wound bled much, but they took their toll on his vitality.

"We can—" began Stine. The man wobbled in the saddle.

"You're wounded. Why commit suicide out here? Why let Villalobos win?" shouted Slocum, hunting for the argument that would convince Stine to break off this ill-conceived attack. They had blundered into an unprepared camp and had taken a few lives. But resistance was growing fast. In the distance, out where they built their bridge, Slocum heard Dunne's voice getting his men to cover so they could mount a better defense.

"Get back!" Slocum shouted.

The men—those who still clung to their horses—obeyed. Stine was woozy from his wounds and trailed Slocum without question. The others, seeing their once-angry foreman riding off, knew the battle was over. They retreated into the night with bullets whizzing past them. Then there were only the memories of the bullets. Slocum found that to be even worse.

12

"Four dead," moaned Abel Stine. "I lost four men to that bastard Villalobos!" The foreman tugged unconsciously at his knit cap, stretching it. Slocum didn't have to read the man's mind to know what Stine was thinking. Plum Creek had been a disaster for him, losing all his men and being scalped. Now he was in the middle of another calamity. He had tried hard and was still failing.

"Not your fault," Slocum assured him. "Those were cunning sons of bitches who opened up on the camp."

"I'm not even sure we got 'em when we attacked," Stine said. "I want to get back at them."

"Let me do it. You build the bridge and get the tracks to the other side of Cutthroat Gorge." Slocum had not led as much as followed Stine into Villalobos's camp. The trail left by the snipers had been obvious. Too obvious. There was something wrong in all this.

"Mr. Atkinson will be back in a day or two. I don't know what to tell him."

"Tell him the truth," Slocum said. "In the meantime, work as hard as you can."

"What about another attack?" asked the foreman. "We can hold them off, but only if we have enough men watching for the attack."

Slocum nodded as an idea began forming. The same would be true of Villalobos.

"This might sound screwy, but don't post more than one or two guards. Get everyone else working as hard as they can. I'll see what I can do. I don't think Villalobos is going to be as much of a nuisance as not getting the bridge done before snowfall."

"We're behind schedule," Stine said, "but not that far behind. We'll be across Cutthroat Gorge in a couple more weeks. It's tricky but—"

"You build the bridge," Slocum said, slapping Stine on the shoulder. "Let me worry about everything else." Slocum got supplies from the cook, then got a rifle and ammo, although he didn't think he would need them. Just before sunup he rode from the C&NM campsite, retracing the route taken by the fleeing dry-gulchers the night before.

Like before, he had no trouble. As the sun came up the trail proved even clearer as it went directly to Villalobos's camp. But this time Slocum noticed something he had missed in the darkness. A faint trail led off before reaching the other railroaders' camp. Brush had been pulled over the trail and some effort had been made to hide this path.

Veering away from Villalobos and his men, Slocum wended his way along deep ravines and into a grassy valley five miles beyond Villalobos's camp. He noticed how the original trail had been so plain a blind man could follow it, but this one required all the skill he had gained over years of tracking to follow.

The green valley looked as if it had been scooped out, leaving behind a gently sloping bowl covered with ankle-high grass and pine trees. Slocum couldn't help reflecting on what a decent place this would make for a ranch. A few hundred head of cattle would do well in this lush territory. With the train only a few miles off, supplies could be brought in from Pueblo and Denver. As the idea came to Slocum, he pushed it away. He wasn't the kind to settle down, no matter how enticing the land.

More than this he heard sounds of distant steel ringing against steel—the same sounds he had come to associate with railroad spikes being driven in to hold steel rail in place. He cut to one side of the valley and then dismounted, preferring to explore on foot to decrease the chance anyone might spot him. The riders from the night before had been confident of their ability to throw off pursuit. He hoped they were too confident to believe anyone from Atkinson's camp had found them.

"Come on, you monkeys," cried a man stripped to the waist and sweating from his own exertions. "Drive that steel. We got another mile to lay today or the boss'll be mad. You don't want that."

"Aw, Vince, what's the difference? The rails don't go nowhere."

"They will, they will," Vince replied. Slocum settled down to watch as they worked to move ties onto the railroad bed, place the rails, and drive the spikes. Vince looked to be the foreman, though he worked as hard as the rest lugging rails and driving spikes.

Leaving his horse, Slocum went to find the camp. Not more than a mile off he found their chuck wagon. The cook was curled up under it, snoring gently. A big tent a few yards off near the trees seemed out of place since the men slept under the stars. Slocum slipped into the tent and saw a stack of papers on a low writing table.

"Well, well," he said, feeling smug in his discovery. "I seem to have discovered the location of the most recent track being laid by Tall Pines Railroad." Documents carrying the company name and seal showed that all the surrounding land had been purchased within the past few weeks.

"They move fast, I'll hand them that," Slocum allowed.

He looked through the legal documents, hunting for one with the name of the company owner on it. The best he could tell, the Tall Pines workers had shot up Atkinson's camp, lured Stine and the others after them, then slipped off the trail leading to Villalobos's camp so the two rivals would fight it out.

Start the fight, then step away and let two innocent companies destroy each other. Then the Tall Pines railroad would either buy the right of ways for a song and a dance or simply take over the track already laid by another company. If everyone was dead, who could dispute Tall Pines' claim that its men had laid track instead of Atkinson or Villalobos?

Slocum didn't know what proof he could find of the plan. These legal documents carried nothing incriminating any judge would convict on. Even Slocum had to admit it was only speculation on his part, but deep in his gut he was sure the killings and bombings had not been done by either Villalobos or Atkinson.

The sound of hooves pounding along the valley alerted Slocum in time to stuff the papers back into their envelopes. He poked his head from the tent and ducked back in. A rider had come into camp, and Vince had stopped work to form a one-man welcome committee.

Somehow, Slocum wasn't too surprised when he saw who it was that had ridden in.

"Esther, you're looking mighty fine today," Vince greeted. The foreman reached up so she could take his hand as she slid from horseback to the ground.

"Did the raid go as I planned?" she asked bluntly.

"It surely did. The fools in Atkinson's camp never knew what hit 'em. We decoyed them out, and they charged right smack into Villalobos and his men. Don't rightly know, but I'd guess as many as ten or fifteen were killed."

"What a sight that must have been," she said with some

relish, "watching them shoot at each other. I wish I had been there to see it all."

The young woman's bloodthirstiness startled him a mite. He held the tent flap open so he could watch without being seen.

"Have you finished this week's quota yet?" she asked, a general requiring a report from a private.

"Not yet, Esther," Vince said. "We're within a mile or two."

"What! A mile or two!" She hit him with a short riding crop. "We have to be ready to connect our lines the minute either Villalobos or my papa quits."

"Why are you doing this to you own pa?" Vince asked. For a reply, he got another lash of the whip. He flinched a little but otherwise showed no reaction to the thin red stripe that bloomed on his chest where the leather had stung him.

"Come into the tent. I have other matters to discuss with you." She spun and stalked toward the tent. Slocum looked around and knew he could never hide. Flopping on his belly, he tugged up the back of the tent and wiggled like a snake until he got under. He pushed down the edge of the tent in time to avoid being seen. But he found himself trapped. The sun shone directly on him. If he stood, he would cast a shadow against the side of the tent that might betray him.

More than this, he wanted to hear what Esther had to say to the foreman of Tall Pines Railroad.

"Have you brought in more equipment?" Esther asked, again in the tone of a boss asking an underling for a report than as a woman to a man. "You were supposed to buy the rail in Pueblo last week."

"We're shipping it any day now," Vince said. Slocum lifted the edge of the tent and ventured a peek under it. The man stood with his brawny arms crossed over his chest. Sweat still glistened on his bare skin. Esther walked around him, as if sizing up a side of beef hanging in a slaughterhouse.

"Are you assembling enough men to take care of any problems, should we have to attack both camps?"

"We're doing all right setting them at each other's throat," Vince said. "Villalobos and Atkinson will kill each other before the week's out. If they don't . . ." He shrugged, as if saying he would take care of the matter personally. Slocum had seldom heard such a death sentence handed down with such indifference. To Vince—and Esther—killing her father was nothing more than an annoying detail to be taken care and then forgotten.

"We are behind schedule. My papa is not. His men work night and day to cross the gorge."

"Cutthroat Gorge is dangerous," Vince said. "We need them to build the bridge for us. No way could I do it with my men. They're not good enough."

"They're not good enough," taunted Esther. "Are you good enough? Are you man enough? That bomb you planted on the bridge was a start, but was it enough?" She ran the riding crop up one arm, across his back and down the other as she continued to circle him. Slocum had seen the same behavior in sharks before they went after a man thrashing about in the ocean.

"I'm layin' track fast, and everything'll be ready when you say," Vince said stoutly.

"You're laying track?" she said in the same taunting voice. "Is that all you can lay?"

She stood in front of him, challenging him. He reached out. She hit his wrist with the riding crop. He pulled away, then reached again. This time Esther did not try to resist. She slipped into the circle of the man's arms and kissed as good as she got.

Slocum saw it was time to get away. Neither of them would notice his moving shadow against the tent if he was careful. He crawled a ways, then stood and made his way back to where he had tethered his paint. The horse stood contentedly, munching at some tufts of juicy grass within its reach.

Slocum mounted and rode from the Tall Pines railroad camp, shaking his head. Things had cleared up for him, even as they had gotten more complicated. Esther Atkinson had not been kidnapped. If anything, she looked to be the brains behind the effort to pit Carlos Villalobos and her father against each other. She would let them rip each other to bloody ribbons, then step in with her track already laid, use the bridges into mining country, and ship ore to Pueblo for a fabulous profit.

Slocum wondered how much it mattered to Esther if her father got his bridge across Cutthroat Gorge built first or Villalobos did. Would she be as enthusiastic about ruining Villalobos? The glee in her voice as she spoke of destroying her father's railroad empire rode with Slocum as he returned to Atkinson's camp.

He had been right about a third party being responsible for all the mischief, but how was he going to tell Atkinson his daughter was the one bringing him his woe? For all that, how could he tell Henrietta that her daughter had gleefully sent a dozen men to their deaths by ordering a bomb planted on the C&NM trestle?

This sent a cold shiver up Slocum's spine. He had almost lost his life in that explosion. He hadn't, and Esther had seduced him later. She was one treacherous filly, and he wasn't sure he could see her again without wanting to put a bullet between her pretty eyes.

Even as that thought crossed his mind, Slocum became aware of someone watching him. He didn't see them as much as feel their eyes boring into him. Looking around didn't reveal who it was, but Slocum knew better than to ignore his instincts. They had kept him alive for many years, during the war and after.

Changing direction suddenly, Slocum cut off the game

trail he had been following and went toward a fall of rock at the side of the canyon that would provide decent cover for him and his horse. The sheer rock wall rising to the north cut off any chance of dodging that way, but Slocum wanted something safe and secure at his back more than a place to run.

He dismounted and found a spot in the rocks. Lowering his rifle, he covered the trail he had just taken and did what he did so well.

He waited. But not long.

13

Slocum's finger tensed on the trigger when he saw Villalobos's foreman and a trio of men picking their way along, studying the rocky ground, trying to track him. He sighted along the octagonal barrel of his Winchester but did not pull the trigger. He could get the entire magazine fired before Dunne and the others ever realized where the bullets came from. But he didn't fire.

Instead, Slocum watched and waited some more. There had been too much killing already, and little of it the fault of either railroad camp. Dunne dismounted and looked at the ground, scratching his head. Slocum had not tried to hide his trail, but Dunne was no tracker.

Slocum considered how likely Dunne would be to listen if he told him Esther was behind the trouble. Remembering that she had been with the dapper foreman in Denver and probably had him tied around her little finger like a piece of string, Slocum held back. Explaining would be a mite harder than showing everyone what went on.

How he was going to reveal Esther for the snake she was, he did not know, but there wouldn't be anyone happy with the young woman after he was done. Clarence Atkinson did not strike Slocum as a pleasant man if crossed.

Carlos Villalobos had a fiery temper and had a nephew's death to avenge. And Vince, over in the Tall Pines railroad camp, was only an underling. There might be someone fronting in the company for Esther that she had similarly spun her web of passion and murder around tightly. She had been a busy girl.

Slocum could not hear what Dunne said, but the men rode on, looking dejected. That they patrolled the mountains rather than working on their own bridge across Cutthroat Gorge told Slocum how disruptive Esther had been.

Giving them time to get down the trail, Slocum finally mounted and continued on his way to Atkinson's camp. Now and then he doubled back to be sure Dunne had not laid a trap for him or had blundered over the trail and was following him. The foreman had disappeared into the wilderness of the Colorado mountains, vanishing as surely as the men who originally explored these lands.

It was some time after noon when Slocum got back to the Colorado and New Mexico railroad camp. The place was well nigh deserted, all the men working feverishly on the Cutthroat Gorge trestle now. Slocum rustled up some grub on his own, then rode down to the end of the tracks.

He could hardly believe his eyes. The bridge was almost finished and Abel Stine had laid down track halfway across it. The engine would be chugging across the gorge in another week, ready to begin turning a tidy profit for the railroad—or at least paying for all the blood, sweat, and death that had gone into laying the track this far.

Stine saw him, waved and beckoned him out onto the trestle. Slocum was hesitant, but made his way out. The bridge did not sway, even in the worst of the gusts hammering away at the structure. He had to hang on to his Stetson, but otherwise felt secure enough walking on the trestle.

"We been workin' our fool heads off to get this done," Stine said needlessly.

"So I see. I've got some news of my own. Is Atkinson in camp?"

"Mr. Atkinson is back in Pueblo, dickerin' with bankers over a new loan. If we can run two locomotives, we can 'bout monopolize the traffic in and out of the gold camps on the other side." Stine turned and looked to the far side of Cutthroat Gorge and smiled. "Not going to be the 'other side' for much longer."

"When will you get the track across?"

"Another day, two at the most. From there we go up a grade that looks easy. Some blasting, not much, then right on into a half dozen gold towns. We bring in supplies, get paid handsomely. We take out ore, get paid even better. Everyone gets rich."

"I hope so," Slocum said, worrying over even broaching the subject of what he had overheard in the Tall Pines camp. He had to say something because Vince had made it clear he would attack if Villalobos wasn't goaded into it. Either way, the lives of Stine's crew were in jeopardy.

"Something's eatin' at you, Slocum. Spit it out." Stine wobbled as a gust of wind whipped through the canyon. The foreman got his footing back and didn't seem to notice anything wrong.

"Let's hike on back to solid ground," Slocum said. He glanced over the edge into a three-hundred-foot chasm. The river—a tributary hurrying south to the Rio Grande rather than west to the Colorado—boiled with white, wind-tossed foam atop the murky green water. If the fall did not kill a man, the raging river would. And the wind! It pulled and tugged at Slocum as he returned to the safety of the notch cut in the mountain where the bridge was securely anchored to the rock just below.

No matter how safe the bridge might be, nothing was more solid than hard rock.

"Yes, sir, Slocum, we're gonna beat Villalobos across. His men can't lay track as fast as we can now that we have our bridge finished," Stine said proudly.

"Things are more complicated than that," Slocum said carefully. "Seems the, uh, people behind the Tall Pines railroad are playing you and Villalobos against each other." He hesitated. "Has Esther been in camp recently?"

"No, of course not. She and her mother are up in Denver. And Mr. Atkinson is making sure we have what we need to push across the gorge. Why'd you ask?"

"Nothing," Slocum said. "I need to talk with Atkinson. We might be able to clear up the bad blood between Villalobos and Atkinson in an afternoon if I can get the two of them together." Slocum did not add that he wanted Esther Atkinson present, too, so he could get her to confess her role in the feud.

That might set off an even bigger battle, but it would no longer be between Atkinson and Villalobos.

"He's supposed to be back by sunup tomorrow with another train of supplies. We're needin' food now more than rail. The boys're really working off the grub."

"I'm going to see if Villalobos will agree to a truce tomorrow around noon. I want to get him and Atkinson together for a palaver." Slocum might be able to kidnap Esther from the Tall Pines camp to get her here, but a lot depended on how close she stayed to Vince and what kind of ruckus she put up.

"I'll ask Mr. Atkinson about it when he gets here," Stine said. "There's too much bad blood for a real truce, but maybe we can stop killin' each other." Stine grinned broadly. "I want to lord it over him that we crossed Cutthroat Gorge first!"

"Keep at it," Slocum said. It was getting toward sundown, and he had a powerful lot of work to do. How he could convince Villalobos to come to Atkinson's camp was a mystery, but he'd work it out. The two railroad magnates might never be friends, but he wanted to stop them from killing each other.

As Slocum rode, he experienced another pang of doubt. Would Villalobos buy it that Esther was working on her own, against both her father and him? Or would the fiery Mexican railroader simply think she had been acting on her father's orders? Even the deaths of a dozen men might not convince Villalobos of that.

"The engine," Slocum said. "That's the point. If Villalobos didn't plant the bomb and blow up the bridge, I can convince him that Atkinson would never risk losing an entire steam engine and that it had to be someone else's doing."

Slocum made his way through twisting canyons along the narrow mountain trails heading in the general direction of Villalobos's camp. The darkness kept him from making good speed, but he remembered how Stine and the others had raced along in the night to shoot up their rivals—and all at the instigation of Esther's hired men. He didn't want to blunder into a trap set by Dunne.

Slocum frowned as he considered Villalobos's foreman. He had no idea how far Esther had her hooks set into the man. Convincing Villalobos to meet Atkinson might not be as hard as telling the well-dressed foreman that his paramour was as likely to stab him in the back as make love to him.

"Poor Henrietta," Slocum said softly, knowing Esther's mother would be devastated when she found what her daughter had been up to. He wondered if she had any idea how faithless Esther was.

Then all his plans and worries faded to nothing. The metallic click of a rifle levering a shell into the chamber warned him—but not soon enough.

"We kin blow you outta the saddle, or you can lift those hands up high where we kin see 'em," came the cold words. Slocum knew this might be a bluff. He also knew it probably wasn't. He reached for the sky and the stars in it.

Coming from shadows, Dunne lifted a six-shooter and pointed it at Slocum. "You got any reason I shouldn't just kill you outright?"

"I want to stop the feud. I want Villalobos to meet with Atkinson. I've got some information about Tall Pines Railroad and what the owner has been doing to—"

"Shut up," Dunne snapped. He pushed his bowler back on his head and peered up at Slocum. "You're the most worthless piece of cow flop I ever seen. This is some trick Atkinson thought up, isn't it, sending you here to slow us down?"

"No trick. Just a chance to bury the hatchet."

"The only hatchet you want to bury is in Villalobos's back!" flared Dunne. "Get him into camp," he ordered. The foreman turned away confidently, telling Slocum he had ridden into a trap. Looking around he saw the three men who had ridden with Dunne earlier rise from their hiding places. All had rifles trained on him. In spite of being cautious, he had still ridden smack into a trap.

Still, this was where Slocum had to go eventually. Dancing around the perimeter of their camp would never convince Villalobos that Atkinson wanted peace between them.

He entered Villalobos's camp and saw a completely different crew of men than over in Atkinson's. These were glum, dour, not laughing or joking. It didn't take much imagination to guess Paco Villalobos's death had robbed them of the will to work—and the engineering expertise required to get across an even more deadly section of Cutthroat Gorge.

"Señor Villalobos!" called Dunne as they entered. "I caught that varmint that's been giving us so much woe."

Villalobos stepped down from a parlor car pulled onto a siding. His bloodshot eyes told Slocum the man hadn't slept much lately. From the slight shakiness in his hands he might even be drinking heavily. He had taken his nephew's death hard.

"So this is the one, eh?" Villalobos said, sneering. "It is good to take this one from my enemy. That weakens Atkinson."

"Atkinson will meet with you tomorrow. He needs to tell you—"

"He tells me nothing!" raged Villalobos. "For twelve years I work in the jungles of Mexico. No one is better at the building of roads through my country. The Mexican National railroad is a miracle. My nephew was at my side, learning and doing better than I could on the bridges. We would have crossed the Barranca del Cobre one day! Topolabampo would have been our crowning jewel. But it was denied us. By you!" Villalobos stabbed out with his finger and dug it into Slocum's chest. "My Paco is dead. So will you be this time tomorrow."

"Mr. Villalobos, the Tall Pines railroad is behind your *and* Atkinson's trouble. They are setting you to kill each other to move in and take what's left."

Villalobos showed no sign of having heard. He raged on, gesturing wildly. Even Dunne, who must have seen this before, stepped back. Finally Villalobos swung around and glared at Slocum.

"The Yaquis are a fierce, proud people. I like them. I learn from them. They make your Apache seem weak-kneed when they take vengeance on their enemy."

Slocum didn't like the way this was going.

"I'm not your enemy, Señor," Slocum said. "Neither is Atkinson."

"He's just goin' on like that to talk you out of killing him," cut in Dunne. "He'll start talking crazy soon."

"Esther Atkinson is the one responsible," Slocum said. "She hates her father and wants to destroy him—and if she takes you down, too, all the better for her."

"See? He's blaming Atkinson's daughter now." The

foreman looked more than a little uneasy. Slocum guessed Villalobos knew nothing about Dunne and Esther.

"The Yaqui, they know ways of making a man's death last days. Weeks! But I am not a Yaqui. I am an impatient man and want you to die soon. In pain for all you have done, but soon. Take him out, Dunne, stake him in the hot sun where he can roast to death. Slowly. But I want him dead by sundown tomorrow."

"Yes, sir," Dunne said. He grabbed Slocum's arm and swung him around before he could argue any more. As the foreman shoved him away, Slocum realized it was pointless trying to argue with Villalobos. He was too consumed with hatred, and maybe guilt, over his nephew's death.

"Watch him good," Dunne ordered his three gunmen. "If he moves, shoot his knees off, but don't kill him. Señor Villalobos has other plans for him."

"I heard," said the tallest of the trio, shivering a little. "Might be kinder to just up and shoot the bastard."

"Or a necktie party," offered another. "We could put the noose around his neck and put him on his horse, then leave him. Horse might wander off to get some water, and he'd never know when that would be. Fitting that his own horse would be responsible for hanging him."

"I know things to do with a knife," the third said, picking his teeth with a huge thick-bladed knife. "I had a partner once who was part Cheyenne. They ain't the most bloodthirsty Injuns around, but they try to make up for it bein' smart. He knew a couple ways of cuttin' muscle in the backs of the ankles that'll cripple a man for life."

"Life's gonna be short for this one," laughed the second.

Slocum settled down and tried not to pay attention to the increasingly vile tortures the three wanted to mete out to him. Getting away with his hide intact was foremost in his mind. He had been a fool thinking any of the men wanted to talk reason. They were more content letting anger rule their lives.

Slocum sat a little straighter when he heard Dunne talking with others in the camp.

". . . attack Atkinson tomorrow. He's about got that bridge built. We kill off the crew when we blow up the bridge."

"Why not take the bridge for our own and nobody will know?" suggested one of Dunne's henchmen. "All they care about on the other side of Cutthroat Gorge is getting fresh food from Denver and finding someone to smelt their ore and buy their gold. Don't matter if it's our train or Atkinson's steaming across."

"Señor Villalobos does not want it that way," Dunne said stiffly. "He will build the bridge across the gorge here as a tribute to Paco."

"Danged waste of a good bridge, if you ask me," the man grumbled.

Slocum shook his head in wonder. Esther might be thwarted yet, and through no understanding of her scheming by the railroaders. Villalobos might blow up the bridge before Esther had a chance to steal it for Tall Pines Railroad. But in this race, Dunne ran neck and neck against Esther. If Slocum had to bet on the eventual winner in this race of treachery, Dunne got very long odds for survival put on his head.

"Villalobos says there'll be bonuses for everyone after the fight," Dunne went on.

Slocum leaned back and stared up into the starry nighttime sky, wondering if he would ever see this lovely sight again. It wasn't looking good. He stayed awake through the rest of the night waiting for a guard to make a mistake.

Unfortunately for him, the guard stayed awake, too, and didn't make one.

At dawn, Villalobos and Dunne came over and gestured. The three gunmen who rode with Dunne grabbed

Slocum and took turns pushing and shoving him along until they were about a mile from camp. The ground was rocky, with patches of dirt here and there.

"Strip him to the waist. Place him there," Villalobos said, pointing to one of the stretches with enough dirt to grow a clump of prickly pear cactus. Slocum saw it had nothing to do with wanting him to be comfortable. Villalobos had chosen a spot where cactus grew. The men ripped off Slocum's shirt and shoved him to the ground. The long spines from the cactus gouged into his flesh and burned as if they had been dipped in acid.

This became the least of his worries.

Dunne carried four railroad spikes. With a few expert blows from a sledgehammer, he drove them into the ground so firmly Slocum knew he could never pull them free.

"Lash him to the spikes," Villalobos ordered. He watched in obvious animosity as the men secured rope around Slocum's wrists and ankles and pulled him out spread-eagle on the ground. He squinted as he stared up into the sky. The sun wasn't even fully over the mountains yet, and he was still almost blinded by the intense sunlight.

"Tighter," ordered Villalobos, as if the men could pull any more on the ropes without yanking Slocum's shoulders from their joints. He winced as the men obeyed. "The Yaqui use uncured rawhide. They dip it in water so it tightens as it dries. I do not have this time to find such thongs. Rope will do."

"You got this all wrong," Slocum said. "I'm not your enemy. Neither is Atkinson."

"Yes, yes," said Villalobos. "It is his daughter." Villalobos sneered at this. "A young girl? What does she know of building railroads or taking lives? She is an innocent. And you will die slowly out in the sun, but die you will."

Villalobos spat on him, then walked away without a backward glance. Slocum craned his neck and saw Dunne with the three gunmen.

He wanted to plead with them to let him go, but he held his tongue. It wouldn't do any good to beg. It only gave them that much satisfaction, and it wasn't the way Slocum wanted to leave the world. He would not plead for his life. He might die, but it would be with his honor intact.

"You're gonna cook out here, you traitorous son of a bitch," Dunne said. "You take a job with Señor Villalobos, then you turn on him. You bring lies about Esther. Wouldn't surprise me if you're not Atkinson's top, hired gunman."

"Watch your back, Dunne, when you're around Esther Atkinson. She's not the hothouse flower Villalobos thinks. She'll kill you if it suits her purposes."

Slocum gasped when Dunne kicked him in the ribs. The way he was pulled taut made the blow impossible to avoid.

"Roast," was all the foreman said. He joined the other three and left Slocum alone in the hot sun.

The hot sun rose and increasingly burned his flesh. Slocum clamped his eyes shut, trying to keep from going blind. The pain grew but he kept thinking of Esther and how she had used them all so effectively.

The heat—and the pain—grew worse and worse.

14

Slocum didn't think it was possible for the sun to get any hotter. It did. His mouth turned to cotton, then his tongue began swelling. His lips puffed up, and his throat felt as if hands squeezed down on it, preventing him from swallowing. But there was no saliva. He choked. He couldn't breathe. He needed water or he would die soon. Nothing in the world seemed as desirable as a drink of water. Cold water, cool water, even boiling water. As long as it was water.

More frightening than the way he suffered from thirst, Slocum felt his right arm pulsing and throbbing as the stitches the doctor in Denver had so carefully used to sew up his flesh threatened to explode. The way Villalobos had staked him out had put a strain on the unhealed wound he had gotten in the Tall Pines office. His flesh burned like fire as the stitches popped open. Every one that snapped sent a lightning bolt of pain up his arm and through his entire body.

Slocum tried not to scream as a surge of panic seized him. What did he gain by remaining stoic? He had nothing to prove. He tried to call out and found himself unable to because of his swollen tongue. That inability to vent his

141

rage and frustration made the agony all the worse. He suffered, and he could not even give voice to it like a wounded animal might.

One thing he did was keep his eyes as tightly shut as possible. What he saved his vision for he couldn't tell. While he still had some strength he had tried in vain to pull the railroad spikes from the ground. Dunne had driven them too hard into dirt and the rock beneath for him to succeed.

When he had first been stretched out, Slocum had thought nothing would be worse than the cactus spines in his back. Now he couldn't even remember the minuscule pain from them. Too much real pain had replaced the discomfort of a few cactus nettles.

Another stitch in his right forearm popped, and Slocum thought he would die then and there.

Drifting in and out of consciousness, he became aware of how the direction of the sun changed. It climbed in the sky and then passed the zenith. Slocum had no hope he could survive 'til sunset because Villalobos would return. If he was still alive, Villalobos would cut his heart out with a rusty knife and then eat the still throbbing organ like some pagan Aztec priest. Slocum's mind conjured up wilder and wilder things as he hallucinated from exposure.

He even began imagining angels. Above him, drifting on the wind, looking like heaven brought to earth. So lovely. Coming for him.

"Pretty," he muttered between dried lips. His tongue felt as if it were the size of his saddle horn now. "Pretty."

"Always the one with the compliment, aren't you, John?" came the divine reply.

"Did you come for me?"

"I didn't know you were here. It's a good thing I did happen by."

"Don't want to die, but you're so pretty," he said, his

mind caught in that thought. An angel was swooping down to carry him off.

He screamed in pain as his right arm suddenly came free. Blood trickled from around the broken sutures. Then he gasped as his left arm came free. He had never thought being dead would be so painful. Pressure off his arms, he scooted down in the dirt a little. The tightness around his ankles vanished. Somehow, in the vast distance, he felt the nettles in his back again.

"So pretty, angel so pretty," he said, squinting as he rolled onto his side to peer at the divine creature who had rescued him.

"You are such a gentleman with the compliments. A simple thank-you would do. But we have to get out of here. Villalobos must be nearby. Come on, sit up."

Slocum gasped as strong hands pulled him to a sitting position.

"Can't we go without walking?" he asked. The words slurred as he worked his tongue and lips and found only puffy pillows. That didn't seem to affect his ability to communicate.

"I'm not strong enough to carry you. Stand up. You can do it. Here. I'll slip your shirt on."

Slocum staggered and stumbled along, being helped by a strong angelic arm. Then he heard a horse whinny.

"Are there horses where we're going?"

"Are you delirious?"

Slocum blinked his eyes hard and got some sense back into his head. Trying to help him up onto the horse was Henrietta Atkinson.

"Henrietta?"

"Who did you think? I'm not some angel come to take you to heaven, after all." She laughed and the sound was the sweetest Slocum had ever heard. "Besides that, you probably won't be heading up when you die."

"I thought—" Slocum struggled to get into the saddle.

Henrietta came up after him, settling in front so his arms were around her waist.

"I'm not sure how far you can ride in this condition. There's a hot spring not far from here. The water tastes terrible, but it might do you some good."

"Need to be out of sun," Slocum said, senses fading again. He wasn't sure if he blacked out, but he was sure Henrietta had saved him.

Warm waters cradled him, lifted him, stole away the pain. Even the myriad stabbings from the cactus spines had vanished. Slocum thought he could live like this forever, floating and dreaming. Dreaming.

He splashed around, struggling as he came fully awake. He reached for his six-shooter but there was nothing at his side. Nothing but wet flesh. He floated naked in the pool of hot water. On the bank of the small pond watching, a slight smile on her face, sat Henrietta Atkinson.

"You make quite a sight," she said. Her brown eyes dipped down to the surface of the water where parts of Slocum bobbed to the surface. He forced himself back down so that he sat on the slippery, rock bottom of the pond and the water came to his neck. He had to float back up, though, when the hot rock became too much to bear on his naked rump.

"I don't remember too much after about eleven o'clock," he said. He bent down and sucked in some of the water. It carried a heavy sulfur taste, but it might as well have been the finest Kentucky bourbon. His tongue and lips felt almost normal, even if he still had a powerful thirst.

"Villalobos must have staked you out to dry around sunrise," Henrietta said. "For a man to do that, he must hate you terribly."

"Reckon he does. Anyone who might have had a thing to do with his nephew's death is fair game, in his eyes."

Slocum splashed more water on his face. He felt better, if not whole, then good enough to keep on living.

As that thought crossed his mind, so did the memory of squinting up and seeing an angel, seeing Henrietta. She had saved him.

"You appear to be feeling better," she said, standing.

"We've got to get back to the camp and warn Stine— warn your husband. Villalobos intends to blow up the bridge and kill as many men as he can. If he can kill your husband, all the better."

"That's important," Henrietta said, reaching to the high collar of her dress. She unbuttoned the top few pearl buttons and let the fabric swing free, revealing the whiteness of her throat. "There's no reason to rush, however. We can reach camp in a few hours if we don't hurry. Or we can reach camp in a couple hours if we do." She slipped her fingers down the inside of her collar. Somehow the buttons popped open like a string of firecrackers going off, leaving her exposed to the waist. Her breasts gleamed white and soft and tempting in the late afternoon sunlight. Then they slid free of the cloth prison of her dress, and Henrietta stood naked to the waist.

"I can use some more time to get my strength back," Slocum allowed. He couldn't take his eyes off the way those twin mounds of succulent flesh swayed gently. As he stared at her, a part of him rose out of the water again. This brought a big smile to Henrietta's face.

"I see my therapy is working," she said.

"I need some serious attention," Slocum said.

Henrietta ran her fingers around her waist and shimmied like a cabaret dancer. The dress slid over her flaring hips and fell to the ground. She stepped free, naked as the day she was born. The triangle of curly brunette fur nestled between her thighs beckoned to Slocum. He grew even harder.

She stepped into the water, let out a low sigh of pleasure, and then paddled in Slocum's direction. Her hands moved underwater to find him. Stroking and squeezing, she worked until he was moaning with need.

Then she kissed and licked along his body, nipping here and softly teasing there. When she came to his right arm, she gently pushed it out of the water.

"You shouldn't get those stitches wet. Doc McKenzie did too good a job on them." Then her mouth closed on his, pushing him back into the water. Slocum half floated, half sat in the pool, occasionally touching the hot rocks under him but mostly buoyed by the warm, volcanically fed pool.

She scooted up his body and placed her knees on either side of his body. His hardness brushed across the woman's nether lips. Then she positioned herself so that he entered her with a rush. They both gasped from the stark pleasure of the smooth, easy thrust.

Slocum felt himself surrounded by clinging flesh at the loins hotter than the water where they floated locked together. Awkwardly reaching around her, he pulled her even closer. Her naked breasts crushed against him. Then they were twisting over and over in the water, splashing about like frolicsome children, but engaged in a decidedly adult pleasure.

Henrietta's legs tightened about him, holding him firmly in place. He began moving his hips faster and faster. Together they slowly climbed until neither could withstand the tensions.

Henrietta gasped out first, clinging fiercely to Slocum. And then he spilled his seed, pumping furiously until he felt both empty and elated. Together they floated in the pool, then began washing off each other until they were ready to make love again.

Slocum eventually pulled himself from the soothing warmth of the pond and lay on a smooth rock, sunning himself dry like a lizard. The heat on his burned body irritated him, but before he could complain or move from the sun that soothed the hurt muscles beneath, Henrietta came to him and began smearing on a paste she had made.

"I learned this a long time ago. Helps with sunburn."

"It's cool," he said. Sniffing, he recognized the odor of cactus pulp. It seemed a reasonable trade. The prickly pear cactus had damaged him, and now it worked to heal his burns.

He lay back, half asleep and feeling the best he had in quite a while, but something niggled at the corners of his mind. He couldn't place it and eventually drifted to sleep.

He awoke with a start. Henrietta had dressed and had washed his clothing. She held up his gun belt with the Colt Navy still in the holster. "Villalobos dropped it not far from you," she said.

Slocum couldn't imagine what went through the mind of a man like Atkinson, turning his back on a woman like this. Henrietta might well be the financial genius in the family. She would certainly have banking connections with her background. And she looked after her man well.

Somehow, it still made Slocum uneasy to have such attention lavished on him. She was a married woman and this wasn't done, no matter the provocation. But he wasn't going to argue too much about it. He took the clothes she had washed and gingerly put them on, being careful about his right arm and the stitches remaining in it. He flexed his fingers. He could still use his right hand to shoot, but if he had to draw fast he'd be a goner.

"You are quite an enigma, John," she said, watching him closely.

"What do you mean?"

"This isn't your fight. I'm not sure what you're being paid, but it can't be enough."

Slocum touched his shirt pocket where he had stashed the reward for rescuing Esther. It was gone. Whether Dunne or one of the men with him had found it, he didn't know. He was no better off now than when he had come to work for the C&NM Railroad.

"I got mixed up in this and want to see it through." He stretched a little. The cactus poultice had eased the pain, but the skin was still tight and blistered in places. "It's gotten personal, too." He started to tell Henrietta about her daughter being mixed up with Tall Pines and then stopped, unsure what to say to convince her. Slocum still needed Henrietta's help to get back to tell Atkinson all he had discovered.

"I suppose so," she said. "When do you think Villalobos will try blowing up the bridge?"

"When it makes the biggest impression," Slocum said. He watched the woman. She put her hand over her mouth and shook her head.

"No, it can't be," she gasped out. "Clarence intends to be on the train as it steams across the gorge. If Villalobos blows up the bridge then, he'll wipe out not only Clarence but the remaining engine as well. It'll mean the end of the Colorado and New Mexico."

"You have any money not sunk into the railroad?" Slocum asked. He saw by her stricken look that the entire Atkinson fortune was riding on the success of reaching the gold fields on the far side of Cutthroat Gorge.

"As I said," Slocum went on, "this is personal for me now. I can't let you become a pauper."

"You're such a good man," Henrietta said, studying him as if he were a unique specimen in her world. "Like I said before, you are an enigma. Hard as nails, yet honorable to a fault. Honor means everything. Give your word, and you'll die keeping it. You come riding up like some wild knight of Old England to save us all, but you're willing to cut down anyone in your way, no matter who they might be."

Slocum said nothing. That was about the way he felt. Saving Henrietta and her share in the railroad seemed the only worthwhile things he could do. Clarence Atkinson was a money-grubbing tyrant, and his daughter was worse. Esther was both conniving and a cold-blooded murderer, even if she did not pull the trigger herself. She manipulated others into doing her dirty work and would ruin her father—or kill him.

Slocum said, "Time to ride for camp. You reckon we can make it in two hours in the dark?" The sun had already dipped below the tall mountains. A chill wind whipped down from higher elevations and chilled him. It felt good against his fevered, burned skin.

"I know the way," Henrietta said confidently.

Slocum mounted, then let the woman climb in front of him. This kept his injured back as free from contact as possible.

He headed down the trail Henrietta pointed out, wending this way and that in unfamiliar terrain. Slocum soon fell into the rhythm of the horse's movements and let his mind slip free.

But something continued to bother him, and he couldn't put his finger on it. He was missing something important. After a while, he pushed it out of his mind as nothing more than a remnant of the torture he had gone through that day. He was lucky to be alive.

He was lucky to have a woman as intelligent and lovely as Henrietta Atkinson along to save him.

Still, what was he missing?

15

They rode into the Colorado and New Mexico camp a little before midnight. Slocum looked around for guards and did not see any posted. He heaved a sigh of relief when they dropped to the ground. But he had the uneasy feeling he was stepping into his own grave.

"Slocum, where you been?" called Abel Stine. Then the foreman saw Henrietta Atkinson. "Mrs. Atkinson, what are you doin' riding around like this? Can I fix you some coffee? Mr. Atkinson's not back yet. Been expectin' him any time, but—"

"That's all right, Abel," she said. "Mr. Slocum's been taking care of me just fine."

Stine looked from the woman to Slocum, then narrowed his eyes. He reached out and put his hand on Slocum's arm. Slocum flinched. Stine had touched the spot where the doctor in Denver had sewn him up.

"You look like death," Stine said.

"Glad to be back. Mrs. Atkinson saved me from Villalobos."

"What!"

"That's not what I have to tell you. Where are the guards?" Slocum gestured around to the empty rocks, all the places where he thought sentries would be best placed.

"We been workin' everyone so hard, nobody could stay awake. That might be a problem," Stine said, "but if we get across the gorge, we won't have to post guards. And Villalobos hasn't been sniping at us like he was."

"It wasn't Villalobos doing the shooting," Slocum said tiredly. He had tried to convince Stine all his trouble boiled up from the Tall Pines railroad camp, but it obviously had not worked. Slocum couldn't imagine what Stine's disbelief would be like if he told the foreman Esther Atkinson was behind it all and that she connived to kill her own father.

Not that all their woe came from that direction. Esther had convinced Villalobos that Atkinson was his enemy and the two companies would eventually fight it out, leaving her the only one standing.

"You aren't tryin' to tell me those upstarts working for Tall Pines are responsible," scoffed Stine.

"Tall Pines Railroad? Why, I declare. That's the most *nothing* company I ever saw," added Henrietta, staring at him strangely.

"There's more," Slocum said, knowing he had to convince them or there would be hell to pay. "Your daughter's behind all this, Henrietta. Esther wasn't kidnapped. She went off with men working for Tall Pines. And she and the foreman, a man named Vince, are plotting to connect the track they're laying with that of your husband's— after they kill him."

"Esther's planning to kill her own father? The girl is headstrong and something of a handful, I'll grant you that, but she would never do anything like this." Henrietta laid her hand on his forehead. "You don't seem to have a fever, John, but you surely are having fever dreams."

"From the look of him, he's been through more than most," Stine said. His hand worked over the top of knit cap, as if remembering how he had been scalped at Plum

Creek and comparing their wounds. "Rest up, Slocum. I'll see to guarding the camp."

"That's a good idea, Abel. Villalobos is on his way to blow up the bridge," Henrietta said firmly. "He is our biggest worry, not Esther. Really." She sniffed like an old woman hearing something totally shocking and outrageous.

Slocum's vitality left him. He had forced himself to keep riding all evening long and had reached the end of his rope. There was only so much he could do. If they didn't believe him, let them guard against Villalobos. Any attempt to take over the road or kill Clarence Atkinson would be met with force. After all, Stine would not know if Atkinson's would-be killers worked for Tall Pines Railroad or Villalobos. And if Esther returned to camp, Slocum would know it right away. That would give him time to thwart any scheme she might have for personally killing her own father.

Slocum looked at Henrietta and wondered if Esther's hatred ran deep enough to kill her mother, too. He could guess that being Clarence Atkinson's daughter was not easy and might engender a passel of hatred over the years, but did that anger boil over to include her mother? Slocum was too tired to think it through.

He knew he had missed a small detail, but found it impossible to concentrate. The thread tickled his mind, then slipped away into the night.

"Rest, John. Everything will be better in the morning. Why don't you go and sleep in my car," Henrietta suggested, pointing to the car on the siding. "I'm not sure I'll get much sleep tonight."

"There's no need to worry, ma'am," Stine assured her. "Mr. Atkinson's coming in the morning. We got the last piece of track in place just after sundown. We can roll his train right on across Cutthroat Gorge when the sun comes up tomorrow morning."

Henrietta and Stine went off, discussing what it might

mean if Villalobos attacked during the ceremony Clarence Atkinson planned to celebrate reaching the far side of the gorge. Slocum's eyes drooped and he wobbled a mite. He went to the woman's parlor car and pulled himself up the steps. Every rung might as well have been an entire mountain to scale. He tumbled into the bed and lay on his back, staring at the ceiling of the car. His right arm throbbed, but felt better than it had all day.

What was he missing?

Slocum fell asleep still worrying that he missed a vital detail.

Slocum was up before sunrise, alert and hurting, but not as badly as the day before. If he didn't worry at his sunburned chest, he got by all right. He made a fist with his right hand and then relaxed it. He could grip fine, too. He might not be able to whip his weight in wildcats, but he'd let them know they had been in a fight.

Going outside, Slocum saw Stine and Henrietta crouched by a low fire, a pot of coffee boiling over the flames. He settled down next to Henrietta.

"You're up early. How do you feel, John?" the woman asked. She clutched a tin cup of the bad coffee, more for warmth than to drink. The evening chill had not left the land yet, although the sun poked a pearly finger of light over the distant mountaintop.

"When's Atkinson due?" Slocum asked, settling down and accepting the coffee cup Stine passed him.

"You're gonna worry yourself into an early grave," Stine said. "We haven't seen hide nor hair of Villalobos's men, Mrs. Atkinson and me."

"The two of you stood guard all night?"

"Why not? The men were tuckered out. They've been working like real troupers. I'm gonna ask Mr. Atkinson to give them all bonuses."

"This is chewing at me," Slocum said, thinking on all

Stine had said. "I heard Villalobos say he wanted revenge and was going to blow up the bridge. He thinks Atkinson was responsible for the death of his nephew Paco."

"No, sir, Mr. Atkinson had nothing to do with that. It must have been one of Villalobos's own men!" declared Stine stoutly.

"It was one of Vince's men," Slocum said. Both Henrietta and Abel Stine stared at him. "The foreman from the Tall Pines camp. I told you, he and Esther are the ones stirring up the trouble between you and Villalobos."

"No matter what he says about Esther," Henrietta said, "I know Villalobos is going to try some mischief. It is curious we didn't see any sign of him last night."

"There's one place you weren't patrolling," Slocum pointed out. "At the bottom of the gorge."

"How's he gonna get there?" demanded Stine. Then his eyes went wide. "He's building his own bridge. He might even have some kind of elevator fixed up to lower men to the gorge floor."

"All he has to do is hike the ten miles along the riverbank, plant the dynamite down below and wait to light the fuse. It'd be dangerous since the entire trestle would collapse on top of him, but Villalobos is a vengeful man willing to take a risk like that," Slocum said.

"I'll send a man down. We'll have to lower him on a rope since there's no way to climb down, except on the trestle itself. Never found so much as a decent ledge while we were working on the bridge. I had to blast a shelf halfway up on both sides to put in the supports."

"He might wait until Clarence pulls the train out onto the bridge," Henrietta said. "That would be the perfect time to blow it up."

"Just like he did before to the other engine," Stine said.

Again Slocum had a curious feeling of missing something important. Everything jumbled in his head. The way Villalobos had almost tortured him to death in the sun,

Henrietta, the earlier bomb blast ordered by Esther, Clarence Atkinson, Esther, always Esther, all spun about in a whirlpool that left him dizzy trying to sort it out.

"We'll go down," Slocum said suddenly. "You and me, Stine."

"Sure, Slocum, but why just us?"

"Because you're the only two men I can rely on in the entire camp," Henrietta said, looking pleased as punch.

"When's Atkinson supposed to highball in?" Slocum asked. It was after 6 A.M. now, and he had heard no stir in the camp of an approaching locomotive.

"Hard to say. He wanted to be here by now, but getting up some of those grades is hard for any engine," Stine said. "I'm not worried on that account. He's got a full trainload of people comin' for the celebration." Stine rubbed his hands on his dirty canvas pants. "What we might find on the canyon floor bothers me more."

"Standing around lollygagging isn't getting us anywhere," Slocum said. "Will you be all right, Henrietta?"

She looked startled at the question.

"Why, yes, John, I'll be fine. That was sweet of you to ask, though."

"Let's see if Villalobos is down there," Slocum said. "If Atkinson doesn't move the train across the tracks, I think the bridge is safe until we check out the supporting timbers." That was small consolation for him as they slung rifles over their backs and prepared to lower themselves into Cutthroat Gorge.

The wind clawed at him, swinging Slocum to and fro like a clock pendulum until he became giddy. He clung to the rope ladder with both hands and closed his eyes. That made the vertigo even worse. Behind him was a sheer, two-hundred-fifty-foot drop. He and Stine had only gone down fifty feet on the rope ladders, but it seemed like a million miles.

"Just a few more feet to the ledge, Slocum," Stine called out. "You needin' help?"

"I'm needing solid rock under my boots," Slocum allowed. He sucked in a deep, settling breath, and continued down. Less than twenty feet more brought him to the narrow ledge Stine had blasted from the mountainside. Four strong supports angled out over the gorge, forming the backbone for the entire bridge. Slocum checked where the wood butted into the mountain and found nothing.

"What would happen if Villalobos blew out the center support?" Slocum asked, peering over the rocky edge the rest of the way to the floor of the gorge. The river ripped along mindlessly, kicking foam into the air and looking more dangerous than ever, should a man happen to fall in.

"The center would fall straight down and bring the rest with it," Stine said. "Especially if there's an engine on the tracks when the center brace is blown up."

Another set of braces rose from the gorge floor to mesh in an intricate pattern that held the railroad tracks safe and secure above. Finding a bomb on these intermediate ledges had been a pipe dream. Slocum knew that Villalobos would hike along the canyon floor, not scale most of the way up to blow out these supports. He had to go down the rest of the way to the canyon floor to check the timbers.

"You got your breath back, Slocum?"

"Let's go," Slocum said, not wanting to bandy words with the foreman. The sooner he got to the bottom, the sooner he could get over his vertigo. Even with such resolve, Slocum had to close his eyes several times on the way down. He felt as if he tumbled backward into space, although he clung tightly to the rope ladder. Going back up would be even worse, but perhaps then he would have the incentive of stopping Villalobos.

As he went down the ladder, swaying and banging against the rock face at times, Slocum wondered if this amounted to a hill of beans. Why save Atkinson and his precious bridge when his own daughter planned to kill him and steal his railroad? This wasn't his fight, except he did feel some obligation toward Henrietta.

"Slocum!" called Stine. "Don't go all the way to the bottom. Work your way over to that stanchion. If we don't cross there, we'll have to swim the damn river!"

Slocum had not considered that. The river formed an impassable barrier to anyone on foot. He and Stine would have to check from above, working their way like spiders along the braces in the tall trestle. As he swung toward the nearest support, he heard the wood creaking from strain. The wind picked up. Slocum was happy to take a moment to cling to the wood, both arms wrapped around the creosote soaked structure.

Then he was dodging bullets. One slug ripped out part of the trestle in front of his face, sending splinters everywhere.

"Stine, where are they?"

"Can't tell," the foreman shouted back. "When I find 'em, they're gonna be dead!"

Slocum pulled his rifle around awkwardly, then settled himself down in the V of two supports, back braced and his feet spread. Spray kicked up from the raging river and he felt eyes sighting him—the river he located. The gunman he didn't.

Until the man fired again.

"At the base!" Slocum shouted. "He's at the base of the trestle." He aimed for a deep shadow and pulled the trigger smoothly. The recoil hurt his sunburned shoulder, but he at least fought back.

Slocum was never sure if his slug found a target because the answering volley sounded as if he had been transported back in time and every Federal soldier had opened fire on him at Gettysburg. Splinters flew like so many wooden insects along with the deadly lead, and Slocum found himself in a fight to the death, most of his assailants unseen.

16

Slocum squeezed off a round and saw a man crumple like a ball of wadded up paper. He swung his rifle around, hunting for targets. From the number of slugs ripping away at the trestle, Villalobos didn't need to use dynamite to bring it down. The leaden termites would gnaw away at the structure until it toppled on its own.

"Where are they, Slocum? I can't see 'em!" yelled Abel Stine.

"Don't waste your ammo. It's a long way to the top to get more," Slocum said. He had not intended to fight a long gun battle with Villalobos. He had thought the rival railroad magnate would send one or two of his blasters with some dynamite and that would be it. Defuse the bomb, save Atkinson's bridge over Cutthroat Gorge. It had sounded logical. He had not counted on Villalobos's intense hatred of Clarence Atkinson for the death of his nephew.

"I'm going to climb higher," Slocum said. He eyed the rope ladder swaying dangerously in the wind. It would be easier to use the ladder to climb up the twenty feet he needed for a better view of the river and banks below. It would also be impossible to grab the wind-tossed ladder or hope Villalobos's men were lousy shots. Dangling at the end of the rope would be like dangling a mouse by its tail in front of a hungry cat.

Pushing up from the V in the timbers where he had braced himself, Slocum put some of the wood between him and the snipers before starting his climb. The sloping supports were easy enough to scale—if it hadn't been for men shooting at him.

Staying as low as he could and making use of the bridge to shield him whenever possible allowed Slocum to climb fifteen feet to the next set of cross braces. Flat on his belly he looked down at the river. Nothing. But in the scrubby growth along the riverbank he saw several suspicious dark lumps that might be gunmen waiting to ventilate him.

Or they might just be rocks.

He set out to determine which. The first shot produced a loud whine as the slug ricocheted off stone. The second shot at a nearby clump gave him a clear hit on a sniper. He had not killed the man crouching there, but had driven him back. Stine started following Slocum's directions and winged one of their attackers.

"How long can we keep this up?" called Stine.

Slocum wasn't about to answer that. Villalobos and his men would hear the answer. All he had was one final magazine worth of ammo. Maybe fifteen rounds. The worst part was uncertainty over how many men he faced.

As he wondered what was the best way of saving both the bridge and his own hide, he felt heavy vibration in the wood that grew so intense it almost flung him into the river below.

"What's that?" he shouted to Stine.

"Train. Mr. Atkinson is bringing up the train."

Slocum did the best he could to find any bomb on the trestle supports. He suspected they had interrupted Villalobos before he had had a chance to plant the bomb, but he couldn't be certain.

"Down below, what's going on?" came the faint cry from the tracks.

Stine shouted out his explanation while Slocum covered him. He was running perilously low on ammunition. Stine wasn't as good a shot as he was, but the foreman had a keen eye and occasionally produced a loud curse in reply to his barrages.

"I'll tell Atkinson. He's got what you need," the man above called.

"What the hell's he talking about?" asked Slocum.

Abel Stine shook his head and looked as puzzled as Slocum. They played a waiting game, taking only clear shots, but Slocum knew this wouldn't work for long. The vibration on the trestle built again, signaling Atkinson's locomotive moving toward the bridge.

"Down below, clear out or die!" came the bombastic order echoing down from the tracks.

Then Slocum was almost thrown from his perch when a cannon blasted out its load of death. The cannonball landed on the bank of the river and exploded, throwing up a column of steam and debris that soared past him.

"He's got artillery!" shouted one of Villalobos's men. This more than Slocum and Stine's firing drove them to retreat. Slocum took a few shots at vanishing backsides but hit nothing. He hung on to the timbers for dear life when the cannon belched out its load of noisy death over and over.

"He brought it to signal the opening of the bridge," Stine guessed. "Never thought it'd be useful for other things."

"Atkinson must have," said Slocum. "He brought cannonballs with him."

Stine shouted for the shelling to stop so they could examine the structure for any bombs Villalobos might have planted. Twenty minutes later, both wet and exhausted, they began the climb up the rope ladder. Slocum flopped onto the solid rock at the edge of the bridge, thankful for something under him that didn't sway or fall apart.

"Get a half dozen men down there. There's no danger. Check the structure. Make sure the timbers are in good repair," Stine ordered. "Keep an eye peeled for a bomb, but Slocum and me didn't find one, so it's probably not there."

Slocum leaned against the rock face of the notch cut to provide access for the train. Atkinson had his fancy locomotive all decked out in crepe banderoles and elegant signs proclaiming the Colorado and New Mexico Railroad the finest in either state and the first across Cutthroat Gorge to benefit miners and the populace of Colorado as a whole.

"This is going to be quite a show, ain't it?" opined an onlooker Slocum had never seen around the camp before.

"Who're you?" Slocum asked pointedly.

"A reporter for the *Rocky Mountain News*. Come all the way down from Denver to see this. Got some relatives over on the other side, so's I get a free trip to see 'em, not to mention a passel of good food and company." The man nudged Slocum in the ribs. "That Clarence Atkinson knows how to throw a party, don't he?"

Slocum walked the length of the train and saw a dozen cars filled with people, all laughing, drinking, and enjoying themselves. He tried to imagine what it would have been like had Villalobos blown the bridge out from under this train. The loss of life would have been terrible.

"John, John!" called Henrietta Atkinson from the rear of the train. She swung out on a platform and waved to him. He hurried to the bottom step and looked up at her. Damn, but she was pretty!

"Your husband's throwing quite a shindig," Slocum said. "Why aren't you taking part?"

"I . . . I don't feel up to all these people," she said. Her brown eyes were distant and from her expression Henrietta thought on other matters. Probably more important ones, considering how her husband turned a simple trip across a bridge into a statewide celebration of his railroading accomplishments.

"I understand why," Slocum allowed. "They're a mite boisterous." The truth was, they were all more than a little drunk on Atkinson's endlessly flowing champagne. He looked around, wondering what was still causing him to be so edgy. Stine had a crew checking the structural integrity of the trestle. Neither he nor Stine had found a bomb on the supports, but they had checked only the lowest levels. Slocum turned and looked past the train, across the bridge to the far side. A bomb planted there would tear out the track and send a train plunging down as surely as one cutting the supports out from under.

"You're worried about something. I heard you didn't find any bomb."

"Might be we didn't look in the right place," Slocum said. Henrietta jumped as if he had stuck her with a pin.

"Whatever do you mean?"

"Don't worry," he told her, sorry that he had sparked any needless anxiety. Henrietta had enough to worry about dealing with her husband. "I'll check the far side of the bridge for any trouble."

"John, what if everything doesn't go exactly right?" Henrietta's hands shook slightly and her expression was now one of focus, a fevered focus that made her brown eyes seem to glow from within with a white-hot power.

"I'll see that it does. Go rest. When this celebration gets rolling, there's not going to be any stopping it."

"Be careful, John. Don't take any unnecessary risks."

He shrugged off her warning. He had spent the day

risking his neck being dangled like bait on a hook over the side of the bridge. The only regret he had about the gunfight with Villalobos and his men was not killing Villalobos himself. It no longer mattered to Slocum whether the Mexican railroad builder believed his tale about Esther and who had killed Paco. Being staked out to die had changed a lot of Slocum's attitudes toward the man.

Slocum walked to the footing of the bridge and stared across the expanse to the far side. The sun caught the steel rails at just the right angle and turned them into twin ribbons of quicksilver. A bomb on the far side would bring down the bridge. He had to check.

First, Slocum peered over the side into the dizzying depths of Cutthroat Gorge. Like so many ants, Stine's men hammered and repaired the places where bullets had gouged out hunks of wood on the supports. Two others moved like monkeys all over the structure, hunting for any bomb that might have been placed. Slocum doubted they would find one higher than he and Stine had made their stand. Villalobos had only arrived and hadn't had time to plant a bomb too high. More than this, it served no purpose to put it up in the girders. That meant a man had to light the fuse and scamper down to the ground and run like hell to avoid being buried by falling timbers and tumbling railroad track.

A bomb planted on the supports would be apparent to anyone hunting for it. Slocum was confident of that. But something worried him. He turned and looked back in the direction of Henrietta's parlor car.

"Why were you out riding so you could rescue me?" he wondered aloud.

"What's that, Slocum?" asked Abel Stine.

"I—nothing," Slocum said. "Something occurred to me. I'll have to ask about it later. I'm still a bit addled from what Villalobos did to me."

"We'll have our revenge, mark my words," Stine said.

"Being first across the gorge will be a start. Mr. Atkinson will ruin Villalobos financially. Then we can do what is needed to him. Make him suffer, then kill the son of a bitch," Stine said with venom.

Slocum turned from the rear of the train to look across the bridge and then back. His head was clearer now that the pain was dying down and questions he ought to have asked before came to his lips. But he had no time to ask Henrietta why she had been out riding alone when her husband had left her safely in Denver.

"Any sign of Esther?" Slocum asked.

"You goin' on about her again, Slocum? Don't. That one's as wild as the wind, but Miss Esther would never do the things you say she has."

"Saw her with Dunne in Denver."

"Villalobos's fancy dressed foreman?" Stine spat. "You were bein' shot at. You didn't see straight."

"Denver," he mused. Something else went unanswered about Denver. He rubbed his arm where the doctor had stitched it up. Some of the stitches were ready to be snipped out. What was it about Denver Slocum couldn't put his finger on?

"You ever hear of the Tall Pines railroad before I broke into their offices?" Slocum asked.

Stine shook his head. "There're companies that come and go all the time. Most won't make it through a hard winter. Others, like the C and NM, will go on and prosper for years."

"Until a wheeler-dealer like Jay Gould comes along and buys it up."

"That happens," Stine admitted, "but Mr. Atkinson isn't going to sell."

"The company has to be worth a fortune now. Why not sell?"

"There are other places to lay track, that's why. We're

railroad men, Mr. Atkinson and me and a lot of the crew. This is what we do. It's *all* we do."

Slocum chewed on that for a spell, then hitched up his gun belt and said, "I'm crossing the bridge to see if there're any problems on the far side. You want to come along?"

"Mr. Atkinson might need me. He's about ready for the ceremony."

"He's priming the pump with all these reporters," Slocum said. Atkinson stood on a rock, hand on lapel, eyes lifted to the sky as if addressing God Himself. The reporters scribbled madly, taking down every word of his pompous, self-praising speech.

"Be sure the men on the trestle below us have gone over every inch with a fine-tooth comb," Slocum said. He started walking for the far side of the bridge, aware of the gusty winds tearing at him. He pulled his hat down a little tighter on his head and tried not to think what it would be like getting blown off the bridge.

A bird could soar. He would fall like a rock.

Slocum turned and looked back, restless and not sure why. On either side of the notch carved in the rock stood an old three-pound cannon left over from the war. Those had driven off Villalobos only an hour earlier. Now they were pointed obliquely out into Cutthroat Gorge and would be fired when the train steamed across.

"All show," Slocum said to himself. He started walking again, studying every tie and every spike driven in to hold the rails to the gravel-packed roadbed laid on the bridge. Stine could have done a better job, but Slocum saw no hint anyone had tampered with the track. A loose rail might have sent the train off the side of the bridge.

But all was secure.

He reached the far side of the gorge and saw a few of Stine's crew standing guard there. Slocum howdyed with them a few minutes and even believed them when they said no one had come by. Slocum certainly saw no hint of a bomb being planted.

All was secure.

"Then why do I have this queasy feeling in my gut?" he wondered aloud. He was missing something important.

What could go wrong?

Slocum rubbed his right arm to get circulation flowing and flexed his hand a few times. It was ready for anything, including a gunfight. But nothing would stand in the way of Atkinson's grand spectacle of the first train—*his* own locomotive—rolling triumphantly across a previously unspanned canyon.

What could go wrong?

17

"This is the big day," Abel Stine said, smiling like a new papa picking up a newborn son. "Never laid track better or faster in all my born days. Never fought like this either, 'cept one other time." He put his hand to the stocking cap. Slocum knew the foreman was remembering the scalping he had endured so many years ago.

In some ways, Slocum felt as if he had been put through a similar ordeal, even if he still had his scalp intact. His back felt all right from the puncturing cactus spines, and his chest wasn't too bad off from the sunburn he had endured most of that day of torture. What festered inside him had nothing to do with physical damage. Revenge was a disease that never went away, even after the reason for seeking it was worm food in some potter's field.

That didn't stop Slocum from wanting Carlos Villalobos dead. Esther Atkinson had a few things to answer for, also. What would be fitting for her, he could not say. He'd think of something.

He flinched when the brass band started up. They played off-key, but no one much noticed. The crowd had drunk too much of Atkinson's free-flowing Grand Mon-

169

opole champagne on the trip here from Denver. For all that, the band was well nigh drunk, too. Spontaneously, the railroad crew burst into "Drill Ye Tarriers, Drill."

"A grand day," Slocum agreed, shouting over the boisterous song.

"Mr. Atkinson is planning on moving the locomotive to the center of the bridge at high noon," Stine said. "Fireworks will go off, and he'll fire those cannons of his. Then he'll come out onto the back platform and issue a statement."

Slocum glanced in the direction of the two field pieces. Their muzzles were turned away from the track where the train would park in the middle of the bridge. Out there Atkinson would be a sitting duck—and the center of attention. One might go along with the other. All Slocum cared about was that no one changed the angle of the cannons to blow parts off the trestle. It wouldn't work as fast as dynamite, but it would be just as sure. He didn't want to think what the effect might be if the cannons were aimed directly at the rear of the train.

Slocum stared out into the emptiness where the fancy train with its fine passenger cars would be in just a short while. The last car was Henrietta's. Slocum wondered if the railroad magnate would share the limelight with his wife. Somehow, he did not think so. This day meant too much to a man like Atkinson to share even a fraction of the adulation.

"You're worrying yourself into an early grave, Slocum," the foreman said. Stine rubbed his hands together in glee. "Enjoy yourself. Suck up some of that bubbly champagne 'fore it's all gone. We deserve to celebrate. We run them bastards off. Villalobos and his gang aren't gonna try anything now. Not with so many people watching. Why, that Mexican sidewinder couldn't get back to Guadalajara fast enough if he tried anything now."

"The bridge might be safe, but Atkinson isn't," Slocum

said. "You don't believe me, but I overheard Esther and the foreman of Tall Pines talking about killing him *and* Villalobos. Esther wants the track for her own company."

"Don't be silly, Slocum. Miss Esther would never harm her pa. They don't get on all that well, and Mr. Atkinson is a hard man, but they get on as good as any family."

"He beats Henrietta, doesn't he?"

Stine turned solemn. "It isn't my place to say how a man and his wife ought to get along. Mrs. Atkinson is good running the things in the company Mr. Atkinson doesn't. He's more of a planning and building man than he is a tending-to-details man."

"She keeps the books," Slocum said. "She also arranges financing from the Denver banks for the C and NM using her father's connections, doesn't she?"

"Can't say," Stine lied. The foreman put on a poker face and stared in a different direction. Slocum read the truth on his supposedly impassive face. "Wouldn't say" was closer. Abel Stine had a real affection for Atkinson that Slocum couldn't fathom. He had to admit it sometimes happened. A partner would say or do anything for a no account, lowdown rascal. Slocum had lost a good partner. He wished he could find another half as good. He just didn't think Stine had found one in Atkinson that matched up.

"Haven't seen anything of Esther, have you?" Slocum asked.

"That's mighty strange, but there's no sign she's been kidnapped again," Stine said.

This was something that rankled Slocum, too. He had lost the reward money for returning Esther, even though she had gone willingly with her hired hands from the Tall Pines railroad. Slocum was coming up empty on all accounts.

"I'll look." Slocum pushed through the crowd of reporters and well-wishers intent on guzzling Atkinson's champagne and eating the fine spread he put out on long tables as he looked for the magnate's daughter. Esther was nowhere to be seen. Slocum wasn't sure if this was good, or if he ought to get even more worried.

His keen eyes swept the higher elevations around the camp, hunting for any trace of sunlight reflecting off a rifle barrel. Slocum doubted Esther would kill her father by asking a sniper to do it. It was chancy at best shooting long range, and Slocum thought Esther's hatred of her father required a more personal touch. He could see her poisoning him or even driving a knife into his ribs, just to watch him die.

Slocum didn't see Esther Atkinson anywhere.

He moved through the crowd, pushing and being pushed like a cork bobbing in a raging river. As he went, Slocum looked for anyone less drunk than the others, someone who might draw something easily hidden in a vest pocket like a Forehand & Wadsworth .32 caliber pistol. Atkinson greeted one dignitary after another. A man posing as a reporter—or a woman with a handbag and the small gun inside—could step right up to him and be sure to kill him.

Slocum looked but did not see anyone trailing Atkinson like a wolf hunting a rabbit.

The crowd was filled with revelers intent on having a good time watching the Colorado and New Mexico railroad break new ground and cross one of the most dangerous chasms in the state. No one had the look of a killer about him.

Slocum began to grow increasingly restive. He felt as if he stood at the bottom of a mountainside staring up at an approaching avalanche. It started slow, then built speed and power until nothing could escape. Running wouldn't do. Fighting was futile. All that was possible was to die.

"Trapped," Slocum said. "I'm trapped and can't get my foot out of the steel jaws." He realized the trap was much gentler than a spring trap and that Henrietta Atkinson was responsible for setting it. He felt sorry for her, even as he admired her and lusted after her. That was a bad combination that made him think with his balls rather than his brain.

"Denver," he said again. Something about Denver and his misadventures there kept nudging into his thoughts. It was so close, yet it slipped away when he tried to grasp it.

Slocum's thoughts were interrupted by Clarence Atkinson's clarion call for attention.

"Ladies and gentlemen—and men of the press," he added with a chuckle. "Welcome to a landmark event. In a few minutes, I shall ride my personal train to the middle of the bridge, signifying the conquest of one of nature's most awesome and deadly chasms. The traversing of this bridge by my railroad shall herald the dawning of a newer, finer day for all Colorado. At long last we will open the mining camps to the south to the genteel culture and markets of Denver!"

A huge cheer went up. Atkinson jumped down and hurried to his car. The workmen had prepared a special train for this trip consisting of the engine, tender, Atkinson's personal car, and his wife's parlor car at the rear. Steam billowed from the engine stack in huge white clouds, and the big steel wheels began spinning on the narrow gauge tracks. Slocum watched until a cold knot formed in his gut.

Something was wrong. What was it?

His hands clenched into fists, then relaxed. He pushed back his right sleeve and looked at the line of stitches Doctor McKenzie had put in and the pink, healing skin under them. Slocum spun and stepped toward the tracks, but was cut off by the press of the crowd. Everyone wanted a front-row seat to see Atkinson's train on the bridge and hear his shouted speech from the center of the previously uncrossed Cutthroat Gorge.

From the middle of the bridge came three long, mournful hoots from the steam whistle.

"Let me through, get out of the way," Slocum said, shoving and pushing. The crowd parted reluctantly in front of him. He got to the edge of the notch carved in the rocky mountainside in time to see Henrietta come out onto the back platform of the parlor car. She turned and looked back, then waved frantically to him.

Slocum never hesitated. He ran hard across the bridge, jumping from tie to tie and trying to keep his balance as the hard wind blasted and tore at him. He kept his head down even when the wind took off his hat and sent it fluttering down to the river below. He concentrated on nothing more than reaching the train. Everything had come together in a rush for him, and he didn't like what it meant.

"John, John, please help me! It's terrible!" cried Henrietta Atkinson.

He grabbed the rear railing and vaulted over it to land beside her.

"Where's Atkinson?" he asked.

"Forget him, John. My husband doesn't matter. It's Villalobos. I don't know how he did it, but he put a bomb on the train!"

Slocum opened the door into her private car and glanced around. Empty. He ran to the other end and opened the door, which was soon knocked back by the sudden gust of wind. Over his shoulder he saw that Henrietta had jumped to the tracks and was making her way back toward the perplexed crowd. The fierce gusts spun her from side to side like a shuttlecock, but she hung on, even dropping to hands and knees and crawling for a few yards.

Slocum started after her, then went back to the door

leading forward to Clarence Atkinson's private car with his thronelike chair in it. Atkinson sat with his back to Slocum, arms precisely aligned on the arms of the chair.

"Atkinson, you have to get out of here. Get your engineer steaming to the other side. Fast!" Slocum rushed to Atkinson's side, then stopped dead in his tracks and stared.

A knife with a fancy jeweled handle had been driven repeatedly into the man's belly and chest. The last thrust had punctured his heart. Slocum knew it had to be the last because that's where the dagger remained sheathed. The expression on the dead railroad magnate's face was a curious combination of shock and pain.

"Henrietta," Slocum said, touching the stitches on his arm. He had figured everything out too late. Then his eyes narrowed as he remembered her words. She'd said Villalobos had planted a bomb. That made no sense since Villalobos had tried to attack from below, along the river, with an entire army of men, and had been run off. How could he have had time to plant another bomb? He would never have bothered with the attack along the river if he had already successfully hidden the dynamite.

Slocum pushed through the front door, leaving behind the grisly, blood-soaked corpse of Clarence Atkinson. Clambering up onto the engine tender, Slocum shouted, "Get this train moving! Get it off the bridge right now!"

Nothing but the sighing wind answered him. Stumbling and falling, frantic now, Slocum made his way over the pile of coal in the tender to slip down the far side into the engine cab, filthy and wanting to be off the train.

"What's wrong? Get moving," Slocum called. Then he saw how Old Irish, the engineer, slumped a little over the open window of the cab. Slocum went to the man and moved his black-and-white striped cap up a mite. A bullet hole just behind the ear showed why the engineer wasn't interested in driving the train. The fireman lay still on the floor. Although he knew the answer, he had to check. Slocum knelt by the fireman and jerked open the heavy denim overall he wore. The bullet that had killed him had missed one of the brass buttons on his overalls and had entered his heart. Slocum guessed both men had died instantly from their wounds.

Unlike Clarence Atkinson, who had suffered as Henrietta drove the knife repeatedly into him.

He had no time to mourn the loss of innocent lives along with Atkinson's. Slocum jumped to the engineer's seat and stared at the bewildering array of dials, trying to figure out what it took to get the train moving off the bridge. The engineer had slumped over, his hand closed on a clutch lever. Slocum hoped this would do the trick. He grasped it, then pulled back, expecting the train to take off like a scalded dog.

It shuddered and shivered and then sighed like wind through a weeping willow's branches.

"No head of steam," Slocum decided. One gauge read only 50 psi. He suspected there had to be more, lots more, before the engine would budge. The whistle blasts might have vented too much steam, and with the fireman dead, there was no heat in the boiler to build up more.

"Ouch," Slocum said as he reached over to open the still-hot boiler door. Flame licked out at him. He grabbed a shovel and began shoveling, but the more coal he shoveled into the boiler, the less the pressure gauge read. Dropping the shovel in disgust, Slocum reckoned a valve was open somewhere. He had no time to find out where.

"A bomb," he muttered. "Henrietta said that Villalobos had planted a bomb somewhere." He looked around the small engine cab and knew there was no place to hide explosives here. If someone had planted the bomb under the load of coal, the explosion would be contained by the steel sides of the tender. A column of ignited coal might sail up into the air and probably kill both the fireman and engineer—but they were dead already.

Slocum guessed Henrietta had something more spectacular in mind. She wanted to blow up the train, the evidence of her three murders, and the bridge under it. Without Clarence Atkinson spearheading the building— or rebuilding—of a bridge over Cutthroat Gorge, evidence of her murders might remain buried forever in the canyon below.

He scrambled back to the parlor car and looked all around Atkinson and the chair he had valued so highly. Pools of drying blood gave mute evidence of the futility of finding a bomb here. The bomb ought to be on top of the blood, not the other way around. Slocum hurriedly examined the rest of the car, pulling open doors and trying to figure out where Henrietta might have placed a bomb.

Then he stopped searching Atkinson's car and went into the woman's. She had free access here and could take all the time she wanted planting the bomb. It didn't matter if the bridge was blown up at the front of the train or the back. If the blast was potent enough it would send anything on the tracks plunging to the river below.

"Where?" Slocum asked, wondering if he ought to follow Henrietta along the tracks. A part of him wanted to save himself. He might not find the bomb in time. But another part of him refused to let the conniving witch win. If he stopped her from blowing up the trestle, he could save the Colorado and New Mexico railroad.

He was caught by a passing thought, wondering why it mattered. Let Henrietta win. To hell with them all. Then he remembered Abel Stine and all the man had gone through. This was as much a monument to his and his crew's skill as it was to Atkinson's bloated vanity.

"Where would she put a bomb?"

Slocum took a deep breath, thinking he might smell burning fuse. Nothing. The wind blasting against the side of the car swept out any possible sulfurous odor of black miner's fuse. He looked around the car, then began tearing at the doors to small cabinets and hunting in any place Henrietta might have hidden a bomb.

"Under the car," he decided when he had ripped apart all he could reach inside the car. Even the bed clothing had been thrown from one end to the other in the car in his futile search for the bomb. Slocum went to the rear platform. The crowd was still assembled where he had left it, but now there was no cheering. He saw Stine standing next to Henrietta, knowing she had told the man nothing but lies.

He hoped the woman stuck to her story that Carlos Villalobos was responsible. If she changed her lie to include Slocum, finding the bomb in time to keep it from blowing the train to hell and gone would only mean facing the wrath of Abel Stine and all his men later. Slocum might as well take the plunge himself off the bridge.

He slid over and stared at the undercarriage of the parlor car, hoping to see something obvious. He didn't.

Where was the bomb? Or was there one? Perhaps Henrietta had been spooked by killing her husband and the other two men.

Even as that thought crossed Slocum's mind, he knew it was false. Nothing in Henrietta's behavior had shown she was flustered. Every move had been carefully thought out—and executed.

Slocum dropped to his knees in the car and began ripping away the carpeting. Running back almost to the door at the rear of the car he found a shallow channel with burned sides. A fuse had already sputtered along.

Frantically ripping at the carpet he followed the channel across the car. Black miner's fuse burned at exactly one foot per minute. He tried to guess where the bomb was, tried to guess how long Henrietta had been gone, tried to imagine what it would be like to die.

The last bit of fancy carpet came free to expose fifty sticks of dynamite—and a few inches of fuse burning its way down to a blasting cap. Slocum dived on the fuse and yanked it free. The shock of pulling the burning fuse away dislodged a blasting cap and set it off with a loud bang. He flinched as tiny bits of burning metal stung his face. Then he yelped as the fuse burned down to his flesh.

But it was only his hand burning. The massive bomb that would have turned the train and the entire trestle to kindling if it had detonated had been rendered impotent. Slocum stared at the closely packed sticks of dynamite in the flooring of the parlor car and wondered if any part of his body would have been found had it exploded.

He didn't think so.

He took a deep breath, then went to the rear platform and looked back at the crowd once again. This time as he started walking he knew he had a murderer to bring to justice. It was too bad it had to be Henrietta Atkinson.

18

"Where is she?" demanded Slocum. He looked around the fringe of the crowd, but did not see Henrietta Atkinson.

Abel Stine pushed his way free and answered, "She took a horse and rode off like all the devils of hell were after her. She wouldn't explain. She said Villalobos had planted a bomb. Did you defuse it, Slocum?"

"I defused it," Slocum said, not wanting to go into the matter with the foreman. "I think you ought to get some men out there and see what Mrs. Atkinson did."

The furor was almost more than he'd counted on. Slocum went to the camp, which had been trampled into the dirt by so many onlookers to the opening ceremony that he hardly recognized it. Finding a spot out of the way, he spread his bedroll and settled down to wait for the questions to start. It didn't take long.

"I'm not sure you have the legal authority to enter into these negotiations, Mr. Slocum," General Palmer said, leaning back at his broad oak desk and puffing hard on an expensive cigar.

"With Mr. Atkinson dead and his wife with a warrant out on her for murdering him, who is left?" asked Abel

Stine. "I'm about the biggest shareholder around, and I asked Mr. Slocum to speak for me."

"Abel, I understand your position," said the General. "Minority shareholders always get squeezed out of such operations. You've gambled your life on the C and NM so you feel, umm, cheated since you received stock in lieu of full pay. However, since women cannot own real property, Mrs. Atkinson has no claim, nor does her daughter, whom I believe is of majority."

"Stine wants to sell the railroad to get the most possible for his shares. The only other buyer might be Carlos Villalobos, and neither of us wants to sell to him." Slocum's hand moved to the Colt Navy holstered at his side. He wanted to give Villalobos more than a sound thrashing. He wanted to see the man dead.

"We might work out something since the rolling stock matches my D and RG narrow gauge."

"What of the track already laid down south of Pueblo?" asked Slocum. "Considerable blood and money went into it. There's even a bridge across Cutthroat Gorge to the goldfields that can open up a flood of money for the right man."

"Such as myself?" chuckled General Palmer. "That's an unproven goldfield. There are men living by eating their own boot soles. Not much gold has reached the Pueblo smelters."

"There will be," said Stine with an earnestness that could not be denied. "Mr. Atkinson knew these things. There's going to be a world of money made running a railroad there and—"

"And all you need to do is take over the line and haul the profits up to your bank," Slocum finished.

"None of my lines is in a position to connect. It is a great expense to connect."

"Here," Slocum said, spreading a map on the table. "This is a map of the entire region. These lines? The Tall

Pines railroad. Esther Atkinson plotted to murder her father and Carlos Villalobos, then connect her road with theirs for complete dominance in shipping. She's gone. Take over the Tall Pines and the few miles of track already put down by them and you have the entire southeastern segment of the state ripe for the plucking."

"How colorful," General Palmer said, eyeing the lines carefully entered on the map in different inks. But Slocum saw, behind the facade of indifference, a spark of interest. For several seconds, Slocum let the railroad builder study the map.

"With Villalobos's line, the bridge Atkinson—and you, Abel—built across Cutthroat Gorge, with Tall Pines Railroad as feeder lines, you have the entire section of Colorado handed to you on a silver platter."

"I would need to consult my board, of course," General Palmer said. "I am being squeezed by the Union Pacific. Mr. Gould is a hard man to deal with. Very intractable. Very."

"I'm sure," Slocum said drily. "However, you can leapfrog him in the south. He either buys you out or he builds his own. And with so much track already in place, could he ever compete?"

"With full scale roads?" Stine added. "These mountains are hard going."

"I am aware of that," General Palmer said. "Let me get some details straight if I am to jump into this deal with both feet. It never pays to go over your head, you know."

Slocum took a deep breath and launched into his tale. "Henrietta and Esther Atkinson might have been working together, or possibly not. Henrietta hated her husband and wanted him dead. She got that. Esther hated Clarence Atkinson, too, and wanted him dead. She also wanted the bridge so her Tall Pines Railroad could steal the route."

"And Carlos Villalobos?" asked General Palmer.

"Esther had his foreman wrapped around her little finger. Dunne was probably an innocent dupe. She was going to kill Villalobos and take over his road—just as you have an opportunity to do without killing anyone."

"She and her mother certainly left behind bloody tracks," Palmer said, shaking his head. "Very well, gentlemen. I shall buy your stock, Mr. Stine, but do not reveal the amount because for your shares I am doubling what I will pay others. Consider this your finder's fee. Should any detail change, inform me directly."

Stine and Slocum quickly left the General's offices and stepped out into the bright Colorado sun. Slocum felt better now, even if loose ends remained.

"I owe you plenty, Slocum. I'll split my share with you," Stine said.

"You worked for years to get that stock," Slocum said. "If you just replace the five hundred that was stolen, I'd appreciate it. If that doesn't cut too deep into your bankroll." Slocum had no idea what Stine might get off his sale of Colorado and New Mexico stock to General Palmer.

Abel Stine laughed. "Slocum, I'm a millionaire, even if Palmer only gives me a dollar a share!"

"What? How's that?"

"I'm free of them. I worked for a snake and didn't know it. I thought the world of his wife, and she turned out to be a cold-blooded murderer. And I don't even want to think about Miss Esther." Stine shuddered. "How much money is it worth to know their real nature and be free of them?"

"Five hundred, in my case," Slocum said. "Buy me a drink, too. I've got a powerful thirst."

Together they found a saloon and got roaring drunk.

Slocum staggered up the stairs in the hotel just off Larimer Square and fumbled with his key. He finally opened it and went into his room. He had really tied one on with

Abel Stine, and it felt good to uncork. Too much had happened for him to keep it all bottled inside. A good drunk burned out some of the hatred he felt. Having the promise of $500 from Stine also helped his frame of mind. Slocum dropped heavily to the bed and pulled off his boots. He tossed them aside, then added his gun belt to the pile before lying back on the soft feather mattress.

He felt as if he floated, soared, letting the wind carry him where it might.

"Too much booze," he decided. It had been a long time since he'd gone on a bender and was out of practice. He closed his eyes, then opened them. Something wasn't right.

He was not alone in the room.

Trying not to seem obvious, he rolled onto his side and let his arm flop over the side of the bed. His Colt was within inches of his fingertips. He scooted around, as if settling down for some serious sleep. Every move brought him just a little closer to his gun.

The metallic click signaling a derringer being cocked froze him.

"You are such a smart man, John," came a voice he recognized all too well.

"I thought the federal marshal would have run you to ground by now, Henrietta," he said. Slocum abandoned his attempt to get his gun and sat up in bed. The woman, dressed in riding clothes, stood at the foot of his bed. The derringer pointed directly at his face. The tiny muzzles looked as big as firehoses to him.

"Him? He's the kind who picks up a snake to kill a stick," she said.

"Where's Esther?"

"That vixen?" Henrietta sounded put out at her daughter. "She tried to kill Villalobos and failed. A pity. We could have taken over his railroad before anyone noticed

what was going on. But when she missed, she lit out."
Henrietta laughed harshly.

"What's so funny?"

"Villalobos's foreman."

"Dunne? The man who dresses up to go to work?"

"That's the one. He's still pining after her. He's hunting
high and low because he thinks he loves her. I hope he
finds her. It would be fitting punishment for both of them.
He's a fool and Esther needs to be brought down a rung
or two." Again the hostility toward Esther came into the
woman's voice.

"She wanted the bridge intact, but you were going to
blow it up to hide murdering your husband and the train
crew. Is that what caused you two to have a falling out?"

"I always wanted the bridge Carlos was building, but
destroying Clarence's carried a . . . certain satisfaction
with it for me. The son of a bitch!"

Slocum said nothing as she walked around the bed and
sat at the foot. The derringer never wavered.

"Esther didn't kill Carlos, and you moved in to deal
with General Palmer. That takes everything out of my
hands now, damn you, John. All my good work is for
nothing. Or not exactly for nothing. I embezzled a great
deal of money from my husband's company over the
years. Some of it went to start up Tall Pines Railroad. The
rest is hidden away where only I know where it is."

"Where's Esther?"

"Who knows? Dunne wanted me to help find her. Ha!
I have other fish to fry. She took what she had embezzled
from the Tall Pines railroad and is on her own now."

Slocum didn't ask what Henrietta had in mind. She
eyed him speculatively, like a cat eyeing a mouse as a
prospective dinner.

"What gave me away?" she asked.

"Other than just happening by when I was staked out?
You knew the name of the doctor here in Denver who

stitched up the wound I got rifling through the Tall Pines office."

"Ah, yes, clumsy of me. I followed you. I was in the other room in the office, the one you did not check. I stopped my men from killing you, by the way. It was just coincidence you found McKenzie. I've known Doctor McKenzie for years and years. In fact, he prescribed my medicine. See how much I care about you, John?"

"Then put down the derringer."

"No, I can't do that. I could if you would come with me. Be my partner. Esther was so weak. You're strong, John. It took a strong man to endure Villalobos's torture. It took a strong man to finish what you started with the C and NM."

"I did it because I owed Stine."

Henrietta laughed and shook her head. A wildness came to her eyes he had never seen before. A wildness bordering on madness.

"You did it for *me*, John. I know you did. Esther might have enticed you, but I held you with my charms. Don't deny it. I saw it." She bent over, her left hand running up the inside of his leg. She massaged his crotch until he began to respond. "I *feel* it." Henrietta laughed again.

She moved like lightning. One instant Slocum was worried about her pulling the trigger, the next she was trying to seduce him. Then her lips pressed passionately against his, only to have the woman jerk back and spring like a deer to the door.

"You and I are on different roads, John. What a pity. The things we could have done together!" With that, Henrietta Atkinson slipped out the door. Slocum heard her light footsteps hurrying away.

He hoped she wouldn't stop until she was far, far out of his life.